Stranded!

The dolphin lifted his head weakly and gazed at Chris with listless eyes. "I hate to leave you, Scamp," Chris told him. "But I have to get help."

Wading out of the water, she noticed a point of light approaching through the darkness, and immediately ran down the shoreline toward it. As she closed in on it, she realized there were two figures outlined in the moonlight.

"I think I see her!" cried a voice that Chris recognized. It was Liza. The other person had to be Sam. Immediately, the two girls ran toward Chris.

"Are you okay?" cried Sam, shining the flashlight into Chris's eyes.

"We knew you'd come here," said Liza.

"I'm okay," said Chris breathlessly, squinting into the light. "But, listen. Remember that dolphin that was injured? I've found him."

"Found him?" gasped Liza. "Where?"

"Just down the beach," Chris told her. "He's swimming in shallow water. I think he's injured or sick. We have to help him. And fast, before the tide comes in!"

Look for these other books in the SITTING PRETTY series:

SITTING PRETTY
A CHANCE FOR CHRIS

by Suzanne Weyn

Troll Associates

Library of Congress Cataloging-in-Publication Data

Weyn, Suzanne.
  A chance for Chris / by Suzanne Weyn.
    p.   cm.—(Sitting pretty; #4)
  Summary: While working as a staff babysitter at the Palm Pavilion
Hotel and helping an injured dolphin, Chris tries to change her
image to attract the hotel's handsome pool boy.
  ISBN 0-8167-2009-6 (lib. bdg.)   ISBN 0-8167-2010-X (pbk.)
  1. Hotels, motels, etc.—Fiction. [1. Babysitters—Fiction.
2. Self-acceptance—Fiction.] I. Title. II. Series: Weyn,
Suzanne. Sitting pretty; #4.
PZ7.W539Cf   1991
[Fic]—dc20   90-11026

A TROLL BOOK, published by Troll Associates,
Mahwah, NJ 07430

Printed in the United States of America.

10   9   8   7   6   5   4   3   2   1

Chapter One

The ocean breeze tossed Chris Brown's strawberry-blond hair as she sat cross-legged on the bow of the cabin cruiser. Leaning back, she tilted her face toward the hot Florida sun. Bright light filtered through her eyelids so that she saw patches of orange and red dancing before her. The steady hum of the boat's motor and the salty smell of the ocean filled the air.

She relaxed as the boat bounced over the waves and wakes. Knowing that there were only two more weeks before school started made Chris cherish spending this day on the water all the more. Chris was almost as excited as she was nervous about starting high school in September. But she wanted these last days of summer to go as slowly as possible.

"Hey, don't go to sleep," said her friend Liza Velez, shaking Chris's shoulder. Chris opened her eyes and stared dreamily at Liza, who stood up and planted her hands on her trim hips. The coppery highlights in Liza's long brown hair shone in the sunlight.

"I wasn't sleeping," Chris protested, straightening the front of the large shirt she wore over her bathing suit. "I was resting—something you wouldn't know anything about." Chris thought of Liza as a whirlwind; she gave the impression of moving even when she was standing still. Chris, on the other hand, liked to take things at her own leisurely pace.

"You can't relax while you're baby-sitting," Liza insisted.

"The kids are fine. We're on a boat, Liza. Where are they going to go?" Chris replied, glancing over her shoulder to the back of the medium-sized cruiser where Samantha O'Neill sat. Her blond, athletic friend was with three eight-year-olds, all wearing bulky orange life jackets. The kids were staying at the Palm Pavilion Hotel, where Sam, Chris and Liza worked as staff baby sitters.

"Sam seems to be having fun back there," Chris observed. "Look what she did to those kids." Sam was a rainbow of colored zinc oxides—yellow on her nose, blue on her shoulders, green on her lips. Apparently she'd shared the small, round tins of colored sunscreen with the two girls and a boy who sat on either side of her. They were all spotted and striped in bright colors.

"She looks like a mother parrot with her babies," commented Liza, grinning.

Watching Sam's animated expression and wild hand movements, Chris knew her friend was telling a story. "I bet she's telling them about the time last summer when the two of you ran into the nurse shark while you were snorkeling," Chris said.

"That thing scared the life out of me," said Liza emphatically. "Even though Sam's father told us nurse sharks don't bother you unless you bother them."

"He knows everything about the ocean," Chris commented as she glanced over at the large, bearded man steering the boat. Sam's father was Captain Dan of Captain Dan's Snorkeling Tours. It was unusual for him to be running his boat on a Monday, since it was the one day of the week he didn't work. Today, though, he was doing his daughter a favor by taking her friends and the kids they were assigned to sit for out on a private trip.

At first, the girls' nervous, high-strung boss, Mr. Parker, had refused to let them take the trip. Though they were good sitters, they had managed to break a few of Mr. Parker's cardinal rules. Star-struck Liza found it impossible not to approach the famous guests who frequented the posh resort. Chris let the handsome pool boy, Bruce Johnson, distract her too often. And Sam, sensible as she was, was somehow always there when her friends managed to stumble into one mishap after the other.

Despite his misgivings, the girls had begged Mr. Parker for days to okay the trip. He'd finally given in after Mr. O'Neill called and said he'd take full responsibility.

Mr. O'Neill slowed the engine. "I think we're in for a treat," he called, pushing back the brim of his captain's hat. Liza and Chris scrambled down from the bow, joining Sam and the kids at the back of the boat. "Look starboard at about ninety degrees," Mr. O'Neill said as he looked through a pair of binoculars.

"What's that mean?" asked Micky, a small, thin Chinese boy who now, thanks to Sam, had a blue nose and red spots on his forehead.

"That's boat talk for over there, to the right," Sam explained, pointing. "Except, I don't see anything."

Mr. O'Neill cut the engine and joined them. "Take a look through these," he said, handing the binoculars to Chris. She took them and did as he said, but she only saw the blue sky and the even bluer ocean. "I think I'm looking in the wrong—" she began, but then something jumped out of the water.

A bluish gray streak flashed past her eyes as it leapt in a low, graceful arch and dove back into the water. "It's a dolphin!" she shouted. "It's beautiful!"

Immediately, ten eager hands reached up to take the binoculars. Chris handed them to a sweet-faced girl with long, blond hair and a green stripe down her nose. "Look over there, Nina," Chris instructed, turning the girl to the correct angle.

"Me next!" cried Martha, a pudgy girl whose face was now full of red squiggles.

"I'm going to move in closer," said Mr. O'Neill, returning to the helm. The engine putted quietly as the boat moved slowly toward the spot where they'd seen the dolphins. "I'm dropping anchor here. We'll sit quiet for a while and hope we haven't scared them away."

4

The boat bobbed on the water as they patiently sat waiting. After a few moments Chris's shoulders sagged. She was beginning to think the dolphins had disappeared. Suddenly, though, her hands flew to her cheeks as one, then two, then three dolphins leapt into the air about ten yards from the boat.

"Awesome," murmured Martha reverently. From Micky's and Nina's wide-eyed expressions, Chris could tell they agreed.

"I've never seen dolphins before," commented Sam, her green eyes still riveted to the spot where the dolphins had been, "except in the marina."

At that moment there was a high, shrill squeal very close to the boat. Chris joined the others in looking over the right side. There—looking back at them with round, dark eyes—was a gray-blue dolphin, his head bobbing playfully out of the water.

"Hi there, big fella," said Mr. O'Neill, laughing. "How are you today?"

The dolphin bobbed up higher in the water and let out a series of clicking sounds.

"I don't believe this!" cried Chris. "He's just like Flipper!"

"Who's that?" asked Micky.

"He was a super-smart dolphin on a TV show. He was a bottle-nosed dolphin, just like this one," Mr. O'Neill answered. He turned to Chris. "How do you know about Flipper?" he asked. "That was before your time."

"Are you kidding?" Sam chimed in. "Chris is a TV

trivia genius. She could probably tell you the name of the dolphin who *played* Flipper."

"I don't know that," Chris admitted, "but that's a good question. I'm going to find out."

As they spoke, they continued watching the dolphin in the water. "What do you think his name is?" asked Martha.

"Maybe it's a her," suggested Liza.

"No," said Micky. "I think he's a he."

There was a murmur of agreement. "He does seem like a he somehow," said Chris.

"But what's his name?" Martha pressed.

"His name is probably Eeeeeee, Eeeeeee," Liza squealed like a dolphin.

"Eeeeeee . . ." Martha tried. "That's too hard to say. He needs a human name."

At that moment, the dolphin threw himself backward into the water and disappeared beneath the surface. "I guess he didn't want a name," Sam said laughing.

They waited for the dolphin to return, all of them leaning anxiously over the side of the boat. The other leaping dolphins maintained a distance of about ten yards. "He's not coming back," said Nina sadly.

"Maybe he swam back to the others," said Micky. But as he spoke there was a splash on the other side of the boat. They turned and saw the dolphin leaping high into the air.

"Why, you scamp!" chuckled Mr. O'Neill.

"What's a scamp?" asked Micky.

"A rascal, someone who likes to play tricks," Mr. O'Neill explained.

"That's a good name," said Chris as they all rushed to the left side of the boat. "We'll call him Scamp."

"Hey, Scamp," called Sam, waving to the dolphin who'd gone below the surface once again. This time the dolphin popped up right below them, squeaking happily.

"He knows his name!" shouted Martha.

Sam, Chris and Liza looked at one another, smiling. "Who knows, maybe he does," said Chris.

"They say dolphins talk to one another," Liza said. "They think someday we'll be able to talk to dolphins in dolphin language."

"Wouldn't that be neat?" said Chris, leaning over the side of the boat, reaching out to touch the dolphin. With the tips of her fingers, she managed to touch his long, narrow nose. "He has such smart eyes," she observed. "I wonder what he would say if we could talk to him."

For about another half-hour they played with the dolphin before he leapt away and swam back toward the others. "Anybody hungry?" asked Chris, sensing that the kids were let down by the dolphin's departure.

There was a resounding "Yes!"

"I think it's time for us to eat that picnic lunch they packed at the hotel," Sam told her father.

"I know just the spot to dock and eat," he answered. "We can even do some snorkeling." He revved the engine and soon they were traveling full speed back toward shore.

"This day has been great," said Chris to Sam. "That

7

dolphin was so amazing. Your father was really nice to take us."

"Yeah, it was nice of him," Sam agreed. "It would be great to go on more trips. I'm a little tired of being stuck at the hotel all the time. Parker is so nervous. Any time we want to leave the hotel he acts like we're going to lose the kids or something. I wish he wasn't such a pain."

"If you want to plan some more trips, you should do it this week," Liza shouted as the boat bumped across the waves.

"Why?" asked Chris, pushing her windblown hair from her eyes.

"Why?" cried Liza in a shocked tone. "Do you mean to tell me you haven't heard the news about Parker?"

Chapter Two

As Chris pushed open her front door, she was still thinking about Liza's news. *What a break!* she thought happily. Mr. Parker would be on vacation for a whole week!

Mrs. Chan was sure to be left in command. As assistant manager in charge of the front desk, Mrs. Chan was no pushover—but she was a lot more easygoing than Mr. Parker. *I can't imagine Mrs. Chan standing by the time clock, making sure we check in at eight-thirty and not eight-thirty-three,* Chris thought as she dropped her beach bag on the large stuffed chair in her living room.

The small, one-story house was quiet except for the whir of the overhead fan. Chris wished her parents would break down and pay for an air conditioner, but her father insisted that the fans were just as effective and much more economical. As far as Chris was concerned, unless she stood directly under the fan, she was always uncomfortably warm.

It was four o'clock. Chris knew her privacy wouldn't last long. Her mother would soon return from teaching summer school at Bonita Beach High. And her father, who managed a restaurant, only worked lunches on Monday so he'd be home soon, too.

Walking through the living room, Chris opened the curtained French doors to her bedroom. She yanked on the fan cord and plopped down onto her bed, letting the warm breeze waft over her.

She couldn't stop thinking about the almost magical image of the dolphins leaping through the ocean. The dolphins seemed to live a life so different from humans, yet so rich. They traveled in groups and communicated in their own language. She knew they had to leap out of the water in order to breathe, but there was something playful in it, too. No one could tell her that Scamp, the dolphin they'd seen, wasn't being friendly and curious. Chris felt privileged to have seen the dolphins, and knew it was an experience she'd never forget.

Rolling lazily onto her stomach, Chris considered how she might use Mr. Parker's absence to her best advantage. When she'd taken the job at the Palm Pavilion she'd had two objectives: to earn some money and to get to know Bruce Johnson better. She *had* become friendly with Bruce, no thanks to Mr. Parker. Every time the manager saw them talking together, he'd find something for one of them to do. "We're not paying idlers," Mr. Parker would huff.

She knew Bruce liked her—but just as a friend. When it came to romance, he had his eye on Jannette Sansibar, a girl from Chris's class who also worked at the hotel. Jannette was a slim, pretty blond . . . with a perky, shallow personality.

Lately, though, Chris had reason to hope. Bruce had been stopping to talk to her often, whenever Mr. Parker wasn't around, at least. And Jannette had been out sick with a virus that seemed to be going around. Now, with Mr. Parker gone, if Jannette would only stay sick, Chris might have a chance to win Bruce over.

"I knew I should have started my diet last week," she muttered. Chris was convinced that Bruce would like her better if she dropped ten pounds.

Rolling out of bed, she grabbed her worn, white terry-cloth robe and headed to the bathroom. "Hi," her mother called from the living room. Mrs. Brown, a short, stocky woman with short brown hair that was starting to turn gray, had a youthful energy about her. "How was the trip?" she asked.

"It was so great," Chris replied. "We saw a bunch of dolphins, and—"

"A pod," said Mrs. Brown.

"A what?" Chris asked.

Mrs. Brown smiled. "It's correct to say 'a pod of dolphins,' not 'a bunch of dolphins.'"

"Mom!" Chris cried. "Here I am trying to tell you about this wonderful thing I saw and you're correcting my language!" Chris realized she was being a little unreasonable, but she didn't care. Being the daughter of an English teacher was a royal pain sometimes. Every time Chris opened her mouth, it seemed to her that her mother corrected her language. "I'll tell you about it later," she grumbled, heading down the hall.

After showering quickly, Chris dressed in her room. She was going to meet Liza and Sam at Flamingo Pizzas. They were going because Liza's boyfriend Eddie worked there as a delivery boy. Liza had heard a rumor that a girl named Donna was hanging around making a play for Eddie. It was Liza's mission to squelch Donna's advances immediately.

Chris and Sam were supposed to be there for back-up, but Chris was eager to go for another reason—she hoped to see Bruce. Eddie and Bruce were friends, and even though Flamingo Pizzas were not the greatest, Bruce often ate there because of Eddie.

She ran a brush through her hair until it shone. Her chin-length hair had lots of body and a light reddish color.

"This skin has got to go," she muttered as she dabbed the blemishes on her chin with medicated cover. Silently she vowed to live on nothing but water until her extra pounds melted and her skin took on a creamy glow.

She put on a black T-shirt and a pair of white cotton clamdiggers. "I'm going down to Flamingo Pizzas, Mom," she called into the kitchen as she headed for the front door.

"We're eating in two hours," her mother objected.

"Don't worry, their pizza stinks," Chris called from the door. "Besides, I'm on a diet."

In a few minutes Chris was leaving the small houses on her block behind and heading into the commercial section of Bonita Beach. Downtown Bonita Beach was little more than several small, one-story shopping arcades, a movie theater, some restaurants, and a few government buildings, all grouped together on either side of a two-lane road. Chris turned into one of the shopping arcades and pulled her bike up in front of a glass-front store with a hot-pink canopy. When she opened the glass door, she was immediately hit with frigid air from the pizzeria's air conditioning.

Liza waved to her from a pink plastic booth. Chris slid into the booth next to Sam and opposite Liza. On the table sat two thick, doughy slices of pizza, lightly sprinkled with tomato sauce and cheese. "Yuck, I don't know how this place stays in business," Chris commented, looking down at the slices.

"It's okay if you don't think of it as pizza," Sam said, picking gingerly at the crust. "Want some?"

"No thanks. I'm starting another diet." Chris scanned the pizzeria. "Did that Donna girl show up?" she asked Liza.

"Speak of the devil," Liza replied under her breath. Chris and Sam turned toward the door. A tall, thin girl with heavy eye makeup and long, dark hair sauntered in.

"Look at that hair. It's dyed," Chris whispered.

"So's mine," Liza reminded her.

"Yours isn't dyed, it's highlighted," Sam insisted. "She looks like a vampire with that hair. Don't worry about her."

"I don't know," Liza said skeptically. "Sometimes boys go for that."

13

"Where's Eddie?" Chris asked, watching Donna walk to the front counter.

"He's out on a delivery," Liza answered. "I asked the guy behind the counter."

After a few moments, a tall boy with dark hair and bright blue eyes walked into the pizzeria. He wore a white T-shirt with the words "Flamingo Pizzas" etched across it in fiery pink. "He hasn't noticed us yet," said Liza, slumping down into her seat. "I want to see what he does." Eddie walked toward the counter, but stopped to chat when Donna called to him.

"That's it," said Liza, slapping her hand down on the table angrily. "I'm going over there and break this up."

"Be cool, Liza," Sam warned. "He's just talking to her."

"Should we go with her?" Chris asked Sam as they watched Liza storm across the pizzeria.

"I think Liza's got this under control," said Sam.

Liza came up behind Eddie and hooked her arm through his elbow. Startled, he turned and smiled at her. Chris knew all was well when he slipped his arm around Liza's waist. "I guess Donna knows what's what now," Chris said, relieved.

"Yeah, look at her face," said Sam. The girl was glaring at Liza with a sour expression. "She looks pretty mad."

"That blew her romantic plans out of the water," laughed Chris. Just then she saw Bruce Johnson coming in through the front door. She quickly smoothed her hair. "Let's invite him to join us for pizza, okay?" she said to Sam eagerly.

"Sure, okay," Sam agreed. "On second thought, maybe we shouldn't."

In the next second, Chris saw what had changed Sam's mind. Bruce was holding the door open for someone—and that someone was a pretty girl with long blond curls. Jannette Sansibar.

"I think I will have some of that pizza, after all," said Chris glumly as she picked up the dried-out pizza and took a bite. "I mean, what's the use in dieting now?"

Chapter Three

"It's hopeless," sighed Chris the next day as the girls punched their cards into the time clock just off the hotel's main kitchen. "It figures Jannette would recover from her virus in no time. Did you see the way she wouldn't even let Bruce talk to us yesterday? As soon as he stopped by the table, she had a million chores for him." Chris mimicked Jannette's girlish, flirtatious voice. "'Oh, Bruce, would you get me another slice? Bruce, I need another napkin. Bruce, be a love and get me some soda.'"

"It was pretty nauseating," Liza agreed.

Chris nodded. "Bruce will never ask me out as long as she's around."

"Don't be negative," Sam scolded, putting her card back into the metal rack. "We'll figure out some way to get you guys together. Jannette's an idiot. He'll get tired of her."

"Boys like dumb girls," Chris grumbled. She didn't

16

want to believe this, but she'd seen enough bright girls act dumb around boys to believe that there might be something to the strategy.

"Not all of them," said Liza. "Eddie likes me better than that airhead Donna."

"Maybe Donna's a genius," said Chris. "Maybe he likes you better because you're not as smart as she is."

"Not likely," Liza snapped. Then she softened. "Hey, Chris, why don't I get Eddie to talk to Bruce?"

"Don't you dare," Chris flared. "I'd die of humiliation." The girls headed through the kitchen, out to a quiet, empty restaurant.

"Have you noticed that it's been real quiet around here lately?" Sam asked.

"I heard Mrs. Chan say that the end of August is the slowest time of the year at the Palm," Liza told them. "That's why Parker takes his vacation now."

"I wonder where he's going," said Sam.

"Probably to a military training camp," Chris joked. The girls had come out of the restaurant and were standing in the luxurious lobby of the Palm Pavilion. Mahogany columns, surrounded by lush palms in brass pots, rose majestically up to the cathedral ceiling. Shimmering sunlight filtered down from the skylights, creating flickering shadows. Large overhead fans turned silently, but they were only for effect. Central air conditioning kept the entire hotel comfortably cool.

Off to the right the front desk curved around. Dressed neatly in uniform blue blazers, the front-desk staff

17

checked the hotel's wealthy clientele in and out. There, each day, Mrs. Chan wrote out the day's assignments and then hung the sheet on a bulletin board to the left of the desk, by the front entrance.

"The assignment sheet is already up," Sam noticed as the girls hurried across the blue-and-pink tiled floor.

"I wonder if I'll have to play checkers with Mr. Schwartz today," said Liza. "When I was hired as a baby sitter, I never thought I'd wind up keeping the world's oldest man company." Hyram Schwartz had been staying at the hotel since June and no one seemed to know when or if he intended to leave. He always requested that Liza be assigned to play checkers with him whenever she wasn't needed as a baby sitter.

"Oh, you mean 'Chas Reynolds'?" Chris grinned, calling Mr. Schwartz by the name he had used during his younger days as a Hollywood stunt man. "I think you're getting to like that old geezer."

Liza had to admit that ever since Mr. Schwartz had told her funny stories about all the famous stars he'd worked with long ago, she'd grown more fond of him. "You might be right," she agreed.

They were almost to the assignment board when Mr. Parker approached them. Jannette Sansibar was at his side. "A moment of your time, please, ladies," called the tall, thin man, smoothing the hair he combed over the top of his balding head.

"I thought he was gone," Chris mumbled.

Liza shrugged. Behind Jannette and Mr. Parker were

18

two other baby sitters. Sunny was short and tough-looking with long, curly red hair, and Lillian was a petite girl with short-cropped hair.

"All right, ladies," Mr. Parker announced, sounding even more tense than usual. "We are going to have a little pre-my-vacation briefing. While I am gone, Mrs. Chan will be in charge. Assuming that only the usual disasters occur this week, you should all be able to muddle through somehow until I return."

"Don't worry about a thing," said Liza brightly.

Mr. Parker's eyes narrowed. "Thank you, Miss Velez," he replied tartly. "From that may I dare to infer that it is needless to worry about your wearing vividly colorful high-top sneakers with your uniform, harassing celebrities, or attempting to best Mr. Schwartz at checkers? Is that correct?"

"Yes, sir," Liza answered contritely.

"Fine, then just a few reminders before I depart." Mr. Parker went over the rules about punctuality, politeness and proper attire. "Should you need an example of what I expect, simply look to Miss Sansibar here," he concluded, smiling at Jannette. Just as she managed to become teacher's pet every year, Jannette had won over Mr. Parker with her saccharine-sweet ways.

"Thank you, Mr. Parker, sir," Jannette said pertly.

Chris was standing behind Liza and Sam. She gave them both sharp jabs in the back to register her annoyance with Jannette. "Ouch!" Sam cried, surprised by Chris's jab.

"Anything wrong, Miss O'Neill?" asked Mr. Parker, one eyebrow arched.

"No, Mr. Parker," Sam answered quickly. "Where are you going on vacation?" she asked, in an effort to smooth over the situation.

Mr. Parker sighed and smiled blissfully. "I'm off to the island of—" He stopped himself and seemed to think better of answering. "Excuse me, Miss O'Neill, but a hideous image just flashed across my brain. I saw myself sitting under a beach umbrella, my feet up, a tall tropical punch in my hand . . . and then I imagined three very familiar young girls walking up the beach toward me, saying, 'You have to come back right away, Mr. Parker. The explosion wasn't really our fault but something terrible has happened . . .' That's where the image fades away. No, I think I'll just keep my whereabouts a secret." With that, Mr. Parker nodded sharply at the girls. "Dismissed," he said, and hurried to the front entrance, where the girls saw him pick up two large suitcases.

"Wow, he really needs this vacation," Chris said as Mr. Parker disappeared out the front door. "He's cracking up."

"He sure is," Liza agreed. "He's imagining three strange girls coming to wreck his vacation. I wonder who they were?"

Sam stared at Liza with disbelief. "Who do you think?" she asked, rolling her eyes.

Liza looked at her blankly for a moment. "Us?"

"Of course, us," said Sam.

20

"Well, I'm sure we'll all do just fine this week," said Jannette, tossing her silky blond hair over her shoulder. "If I can be of any help, you all let me know."

Sam, Liza and Chris nodded at Jannette with phony smiles. Sunny, Lillian and Jannette went off to pick up the children they would be sitting for that day.

"Ooohh, she bugs me so much," Chris grumbled.

"She's so icky-sweet she gives me a toothache," Liza added.

The three girls checked the assignment sheet and discovered that they'd be sitting for Micky, Nina and Martha again. "Good, they're easy," noted Chris.

When they'd picked the kids up, they took them outside to the largest of the hotel's three pools. Since the three children had gotten to know one another the day before, they began playing together right away. Liza, Chris and Sam sat at the edge of the pool and watched as the kids tossed a beach ball in a three-way catch.

The sun sparkled on the water and a breeze blew up from the ocean at their backs. "You know, I've got an idea," said Sam after a while. "If we threw a party, it might be a good way for Chris to get to talk to Bruce."

Chris's eyes lit up. "That's a great idea! We'll throw a party and—"

"—and not invite Jannette," Liza finished.

"Is that too mean?" Chris asked.

"No," Liza insisted. "She wouldn't invite us to a party

if she were having one. We know her, but we're not friends with her or anything."

"That's true," Sam agreed. "Let's do it. When should we have the party?"

"As soon as possible!" said Chris excitedly.

Chapter Four

That afternoon, the girls were eager to begin planning their party. They rushed for the time clock as soon as their shift ended. As they punched out, Chris noticed Mrs. Chan coming up behind them. *Wow, she looks awful*, thought Chris, noticing the petite woman's chalky complexion and listless eyes.

"Are you okay?" she asked as Mrs. Chan punched out. "You don't look so hot."

"Hot is exactly what I feel," Mrs. Chan replied. "I have a fever and my body aches. That's why I'm leaving so early."

"I bet you have that virus everyone's catching," Sam suggested.

"No doubt," agreed Mrs. Chan, fishing her car keys from her white leather bag. "All I want is to get home and crawl into bed."

"What should we do if you're not here tomorrow?" Liza asked as Mrs. Chan slowly headed out the door.

23

"I'll be here," Mrs. Chan replied wearily. "With Mr. Parker gone, I don't have any choice."

"Poor Mrs. Chan," said Sam when the woman had gone. "She looked like she was about to keel over."

"Come on, let's go," Chris hurried Liza and Sam along. They went out, unchained their bikes and rode away from the hotel. No matter how many times Chris made the change from the world of the Palm Pavilion back to the rest of Bonita Beach, her reaction was the same. She had the vague feeling that she'd dreamed up the Palm Pavilion and it wasn't real at all. How could there really be a place with gold fixtures in its luxury suites, three pools and the ocean in its backyard? The Palm's guests all looked as if they'd stepped out of fashion magazines. Surely it had to be a dream.

Riding out onto the dusty road made the Palm seem all the more dreamlike. Bonita Beach was nothing like that world. The one other hotel it boasted was the Sleep-Ezy, which was almost out of town. The only people Chris knew of who stayed there were fishermen who came down to rent boats and go game fishing.

Unlike Liza and Sam, Chris liked Bonita Beach. Liza had her heart set on going to Hollywood as soon as she was eighteen. Sometimes Chris felt as if, in her mind, Liza had already left the beach town behind.

Sam also hoped to find fame and fortune—as a professional athlete. And her dreams of competing in the Olympics—she wasn't sure for which sport yet—would certainly take her far away from her hometown.

But for Chris, living in this small town by the ocean gave her a sense of completeness that nothing else could. She really couldn't imagine calling any other place home.

The girls biked down the road through the center of town, and turned right into a residential section of small wooden and stucco homes. Earlier they had agreed to hold the party at Sam's. Though her house wasn't any larger than Chris's or Liza's, she had the biggest yard. Chris followed Sam and Liza up the dirt path that led to Sam's white house.

Sam leaned her bike against the wide steps leading up to the front porch. A black Labrador retriever bounded out the screen door, nearly knocking Sam off her feet as he jumped up to greet her. "Hi, Trevor." Sam laughed as the dog licked her face happily.

"Is all this dog food for Trevor?" asked Liza, laying her bike on the ground near Sam's.

As Chris got off her bike, she saw what Liza was referring to. Sam's porch was stacked high with large orange bags marked "Chompy Pet."

"It is now," Sam remarked.

"Wasn't your mother in business trying to sell this stuff?" asked Chris, vaguely remembering Sam telling her about her mother's most recent business venture.

Sam checked over her shoulder. "Yep," she said in a low tone. "And before that she tried to sell cleaning products. We still have a ton of them in the garage. She's not the greatest saleswoman."

At that moment, a pretty woman with red hair that

fell in loose curls to her shoulders came out onto the porch. If it weren't for the wrinkles around her green eyes, she would have looked like a college girl, dressed as she was in a T-shirt and cut-off jeans.

"Hi, Mom," said Sam. "Would it be okay if I had a party here?"

"I think so," Mrs. O'Neill replied. "When?"

Sam looked at Chris. *The sooner the better*, thought Chris.

"This Saturday?" Sam asked hesitantly.

"Fine with me," said her mother.

"Think we can do it that fast?" Chris asked Liza and Sam.

"Why not?" Liza replied. "Today's only Tuesday."

"No more than twenty people, though," Sam's mother told them as she stepped down off the porch. She whistled sharply for Trevor, and headed down the dirt path with the dog bounding alongside her.

Just then, a blue, rust-splotched car with a noisy muffler pulled up. "I can't believe your sister's old bomb is still going," said Liza, sitting cross-legged on the porch.

"Every time she goes for a drive something else seems to fall apart," Sam noted. "Greta doesn't care as long as it rolls."

Sam's seventeen-year-old sister worked as a lunch waitress at the Palm Pavilion. She climbed out of the car dressed in the A-line black polyester dress all the waitresses wore, but was carrying her shoes so she could walk barefoot. Her long, bleached-blond hair was a little wavy from being tied in a bun all day.

Greta's boyfriend, Lloyd, a tall, muscular nineteen-year-old, got out of the passenger seat of the car. He had white-blond hair that flopped into his eyes and a perfectly even tan that he showed off by wearing a bright yellow tank top and white shorts.

"Hey, did you hear Parker went on vacation?" Greta asked the three girls as she climbed the front steps.

"Yeah, we're planning a celebration party right now," Liza answered. "And we're inviting all our friends."

"Oh, no, there'll be little teenyboppers running all over this place!" Greta moaned. "The whole house will smell like zit cream."

"Go bleach your roots, Greta," Sam shot back.

Greta reached up to touch her hair. "Oh, very funny, Samantha," she snapped after a moment. She yanked the door open and went into the house, letting the door slam shut behind her.

Lloyd came up the stairs, yawned, and stretched out on the wooden bench near the door, his long legs sprawled in front of him.

"Tough day surfing, Lloyd?" asked Sam with more than a hint of sarcasm.

Chris smiled at Sam's comment. She thought it was funny the way Lloyd irked Sam. Lloyd seemed perfectly nice to Chris. But whenever she voiced that opinion, Sam would roll her eyes and say something like, "You wouldn't think so if you had to push him aside every time you wanted some food from your own refrigerator."

Whether intentionally, or through sheer spaciness, Lloyd never picked up on Sam's ironic cracks. "It *was* a tough day," he answered earnestly. "The waves weren't breaking at all. Man, someday I'm going to Hawaii where they have, like, tidal waves every day."

"You better keep playing that Winning Jackpot game, if you want to get to Hawaii," said Sam.

"Yeah, good idea," said Lloyd absently. "So, are you guys really planning a bash?" he asked.

"Definitely," Liza replied. "Are you coming?"

Before Sam could object, a van pulled up to the house and her father got out. "What's he doing home so early?" Sam wondered out loud.

Mr. O'Neill headed up to the house. "What's up?" Sam asked.

"I didn't have enough bookings to make it worth running an afternoon tour," he answered. "End of August is always slow." He took off his captain's hat and rumpled his thick, dark hair. "Any phone calls for me?"

"I don't know. We just got here," Sam told him.

Greta came back onto the porch wearing shorts and a T-shirt. "A guy named Artie Howard just called you," she told her father. "I didn't know you were home."

"I said I'd go back down to the marina and help him repair his outboard motor. He hit something today. He's afraid it might have been one of the dolphins we saw yesterday."

"Oh, no!" cried Liza.

Mr. O'Neill nodded. "The dolphin surprised him and came right up near the boat as he was turning. Almost scared him to death."

"If the outboard is busted, then the dolphin must be hurt, too," said Sam.

"Probably," her father agreed sadly.

"I bet it was Scamp," said Chris, feeling a lump forming in her throat. "I hope he's okay."

Chapter Five

The next morning, Chris found herself still thinking about Scamp. *What do dolphins do when they're injured?* she wondered, letting the warm water from the shower pound on her shoulders. She remembered the creature's playful manner. Something about the dolphin had touched her heart and she couldn't bear to think of it in pain.

Chris wrapped her wet hair in a towel and quickly slipped into a pair of khaki shorts and her Palm Pavilion polo shirt. "Oh, the dolphin is probably fine," she told herself. "I'm worrying for nothing. That guy is just guessing that he hit it."

She leaned into the mirror over the sink and applied a light coat of medicated cover on her chin and forehead, then added some blush. "I'll never have cheekbones," she said with a sigh. She broke the seal on the plum-colored mascara she'd bought the day before. *Yuck*, she thought, after applying it to one eye. *It makes me look like I have pinkeye or some other disease.*

There was a quick rap on the door. "It's almost eight!" her father called. "I have to get in there."

"I'm coming," she shouted back.

A few moments later she grabbed her bike from the porch steps and went to pick up Liza. Chris was late, so she wasn't surprised to find Liza already straddling her bike, ready to go.

Together they rode to Sam's house. From there, the three of them biked together to the Palm Pavilion. It wasn't yet eight-thirty and already the temperature was in the nineties—the day was going to be a scorcher.

Chris wiped perspiration from her brow and pedaled faster around the bend right before the Palm Pavilion. With its rose-colored walls and crisp, white awnings, the hotel seemed immune to the Florida sun. No matter how still the air was in town, at the hotel there was always a refreshing ocean breeze rustling the palm trees that lined its long, winding front drive.

As they chained their bikes in the rack at the side of the hotel, Chris hesitated. "Does my face look too bad?" she asked Sam and Liza.

"No worse than usual," Sam teased.

"I mean my skin," Chris said anxiously. She didn't want to run into Bruce looking like a mass of pimples.

"Your skin doesn't look too bad," said Liza, looking at Chris closely. "But is something the matter with your right eye? I just noticed that it's pink around the outside."

31

Chris clapped her hand over her eye. "That stupid plum mascara. Why did you tell me to buy it?"

"I only said it might look good. You're the one who bought it!" Liza defended herself.

"Come on. Don't stand here arguing. We're late already," said Sam.

Liza checked her watch. "It's only eight-thirty-five. Relax. Parker is gone and Mrs. Chan will be too busy to notice. She may even be out sick."

"You're right. I forgot," said Sam. "We might as well enjoy the freedom while we can."

"No kidding," Liza agreed. "We have from now until next Tuesday, when Parker returns. We've worked hard all summer. We deserve a break."

"What about my eye?" Chris asked.

"It's hardly noticeable," said Liza. "Besides, with Parker gone, we'll have time to fix it in the ladies' room."

"That's true," Chris said, relieved. The girls ambled toward the hotel's service entrance. It was a great feeling to know that Mr. Parker wouldn't be standing by the time clock, his toe tapping irritably just because they were a few minutes late.

"It's not like I plan to goof off or anything," said Liza. "But we won't have to worry about every little rule. Why should we have to punch in at the stroke of eight-thirty? The assignment list never goes up until eight-forty-five."

"Parker says he wants to make sure everyone is ready to get right to work as soon as the list goes up," said Sam.

"I know," admitted Liza grudgingly, "but who cares if

32

you're there fifteen minutes early or five minutes early?"

"They do pay us from eight-thirty," Chris pointed out.

"Well, I think we deserve one week of living like normal people without Parker breathing down our necks," Liza insisted. "I may even wear my new purple feather earrings tomorrow."

"Parker would hate those," Chris giggled mischievously. "I might not bother to iron my shorts," she added, beginning to feel elated at their newfound freedom. "What will you do, Sam?"

"I don't know," Sam replied thoughtfully. "Maybe I'll . . . wear yellow socks."

"Excellent," laughed Liza. "Parker would freak!"

The girls walked through the side screen door into the hallway and punched the clock. Their time cards said eight-thirty-eight. It was strangely thrilling to know that there would be no one to scold them. Mrs. Chan didn't get upset about such petty things.

Liza lifted Mrs. Chan's card out of its slot. The words "Wed.—called in sick" were handwritten in, probably by one of the secretaries in the accounting office who would have gotten the message.

"I hope she's okay," said Chris, looking over Liza's shoulder.

"It's just that bug everyone's got," Liza said confidently. "Meanwhile we have no boss until she gets better. Maybe we can even leave a little early today and work on the party."

"Yeah," Chris agreed eagerly. "We could finish our invitation calls." They'd begun inviting friends from

Sam's house the afternoon before, but Mrs. O'Neill had called Sam for dinner, so they'd decided to try the rest of their friends today.

Chris, Sam and Liza sauntered out of the kitchen and through the restaurant. "I'm going to the bathroom to fix my eye," Chris said.

"I'll go with you," said Liza. "I have some eye makeup in my bag. I'll line your eyes for you."

"I'll come too, I guess," said Sam.

They were heading for the ladies' room to the right of the main lobby when, suddenly, a woman with pale skin and short, almost jet-black hair blocked their path. She was at least six feet tall.

Chris had never seen her before, so she was surprised that the woman wore the neat blue blazer of the front-desk staff. "Going somewhere, girls?" she asked in a commanding voice.

"To the bathroom," Chris answered, looking at Sam and Liza quizzically. Who was this woman? Did they have to answer her?

"I think not," the woman said sharply.

"If we have to go to the bathroom, we have to go," Liza said.

"Is that so," said the woman, stepping back to study Liza with small, dark eyes. "Perhaps you should have taken care of that between eight-thirty and eight-forty-four." She checked a narrow black wristwatch. "It is now eight-forty-five. I suggest you get to the assignment sheet immediately if you value your jobs."

"Excuse me, but who are you?" Sam ventured.

34

"I am Miss Peabody, Assistant Divisional Vice President with the Highcourt Group," the woman answered with pride.

Liza and Sam looked perplexed. "They're the big company that owns the Palm, aren't they?" Chris said, remembering overhearing Mrs. Chan and Mr. Parker talking about the big bosses at Highcourt.

"Precisely," replied Miss Peabody, impressed that Chris knew about the company. "I will be filling in for Mrs. Chan while she's ill. I was here for an efficiency check anyway."

"Oh," said Sam pleasantly. "Then welcome to the Palm Pavilion."

Miss Peabody frowned. "Don't attempt to smooth over your lateness with glibness, young lady," she said. "And what is that on your sneaker?"

Chris looked quickly at Sam's white sneakers. There was nothing wrong with them that she could see. "There is dirt on your right heel," Miss Peabody pointed out.

"It's from my bicycle chain," Sam said. She bent down and wiped away the stripe of black grease.

"For as long as you represent the Palm, I suggest you be more concerned about your personal grooming," said Miss Peabody unpleasantly. "Now, you girls march to that assignment board and let's have no more goldbricking."

"Gold what?" asked Liza under her breath as they headed across the lobby for the assignment board.

"It means goofing off," Sam told her.

"How did she even know who we were?" Chris wondered, sneaking a peek over at Miss Peabody, who had returned to the front desk.

"She's Miss Efficiency. I guess she knows everything," Liza grumbled.

Chris's shoulders slumped. So much for their wonderful week of freedom.

Chapter Six

Chris hadn't felt as tense at work since her very first week at the Palm. Every time she turned around, it seemed as if Miss Peabody's beady eyes were on her.

That day Chris was baby-sitting alone at the pool. Sam and Liza were swimming in the ocean with Martha and Nina. Chris had Micky, who was preparing for his intermediate swimmer's test and had to practice his underwater swimming. Before Micky had even gotten into the pool, Miss Peabody had stopped by to criticize Chris's posture—telling her, "The Palm staff does not slump around."

Ten minutes later, she came back, ordering Chris to throw away the cup of water she was drinking. "Palm staff does not eat or drink while on duty," she'd said.

"It's just water," Chris had objected. She was counting on a steady intake of water to help fight the hunger she was experiencing on her diet. Besides, she'd never heard of this rule before. If such a rule existed, Mr. Parker didn't enforce it.

At Chris's words Miss Peabody had straightened up like a sergeant. "I don't tolerate back talk from the staff, Brown. Get rid of that cup."

Once a whole half-hour had passed without any sign of Miss Peabody, Chris became optimistic that she'd seen the last of her for the day. Little by little she began to relax and enjoy herself as she watched Micky swim beneath the surface of the crystal-clear water.

She was lying by the side of the pool, carefully counting how many seconds Micky could stay underwater, when Mrs. Peabody returned. "Look alive, Brown!" she barked. "You're not here to sunbathe. Where is the child in your care?"

Chris sat up straight. At that moment Micky surged up from the water, gasping for air. "How long?" he asked breathlessly.

"Sorry, Micky. I lost count," Chris admitted.

The boy slapped the water, annoyed. "That was my record-breaker. I know it was."

"Sorry, Micky."

"It seems you should be more attentive to your work," Miss Peabody observed tartly.

Chris felt her temper rise. If Miss Peabody hadn't disturbed her, she would have known exactly how long Micky had been underwater. "I lost count when you arrived, Miss Peabody," Chris explained, trying not to raise her voice in anger.

"It is a weak-minded person who blames her failures

38

on another, Brown," preached Miss Peabody, walking away. "Now pay attention to that child."

Chris inhaled deeply.

Thinking it might be best to steer clear of the woman, Chris stood up. "Want to go for a walk, Micky?" she called down to the boy.

"Cool," he agreed, scrambling up the side of the pool and shaking the water from his black bangs.

Chris and Micky spent the afternoon combing the seashore, looking for shells. At about one-thirty they headed back to the hotel.

Micky immediately headed for Sal's snack bar by the pool. Chris ordered a chili dog and a root beer for him and paid for it with the money his mother had given her. "There's my mom now," Micky cried as Chris went to hand him his food.

A tall Chinese woman approached them, her flowered beach cover-up flowing around her matching bathing suit. "There you are, sweetheart. I've been looking for you," she said.

"Is anything wrong?" Chris asked.

"Not at all," said the woman. "I've simply contacted a dear friend of mine who's going to take Micky and me to lunch."

"That's great," said Chris politely.

"Sounds boring to me," Micky piped up. "Guess what, Mom. I found all these shells!" Micky offered his mother his plastic bag filled with the morning's treasures. "We had a great time. Look at all this stuff."

"How lovely," said the woman, clearly pleased that her

son had had such a good time. She reached into the pocket of her cover-up and pulled out a neatly folded bill. "This is for you," she said as she pressed the money into Chris's hand. "We're leaving this evening. Micky has had the most wonderful time and it's all because of you."

"I'm glad to hear that. He's a nice boy," Chris replied sincerely. She peeked at the money in her hand. It was a twenty-dollar bill! They were forbidden to accept tips—but twenty dollars was a lot of money. She'd have to work an entire shift to earn that. . . . No, she couldn't take it. It was against the rules.

"Thank you, but I'm not allowed to accept tips," she said reluctantly, handing Micky's mother back the bill.

"All right," said the woman, pocketing the money. "But I do appreciate your help."

"It was my pleasure," Chris replied graciously. "Oh, your lunch," she said, offering Micky the chili dog.

"It will spoil his appetite. You keep it," said his mother.

When Micky and his mother had left, Chris sat down on one of the beach chairs. *I'm really getting good at this job*, she thought, pleased with herself. When she'd first taken it, she wasn't confident that she could handle the work. *Now look at me*, she told herself. *I didn't even take a twenty-dollar tip for it. Who'd have dreamed I'd turn into an almost-model employee.*

She leaned back in the chair and stretched. *Since I'm being the model employee today, I suppose that I should go see if they have anything for me to do until two o'clock*, she decided. Her stomach rumbled. The chili dog and soda sure looked good. *Be strong, Christine,* she urged herself. *But what harm could one little bite do? I'll take a little nibble and then go see if there's any work for me before I leave.*

At that moment, the inspiration she needed to stick with her diet arrived. Bruce Johnson appeared, carrying a pile of chairs that he began to set out around the pool area. He worked without looking up, not at all self-conscious about his good looks.

Hey, maybe he'd like a chili dog, thought Chris, getting up from her chair. This was a perfect opportunity. Since she was heading up to the hotel anyway, it was completely natural for her to pass him.

"Hi," she called when she was near enough. "I inherited an untouched chili dog and a soda. Interested in a snack?"

"Don't you want it?" he asked with a dazzling white smile.

"I don't really like chili," Chris fibbed, not about to tell him that she was dieting.

"Thanks," Bruce said, biting into the dog. "I'm starved and that Miss Pea-Brain has kept me so busy I haven't even had a chance to take my crummy fifteen-minute break."

Chris laughed. "She's horrible, isn't she?"

"She makes Parker seem like Santa Claus," Bruce agreed, gulping down the soda.

It's so easy to talk to him, thought Chris. *He's not like any other boy in the world.* At first Chris had been smitten with his looks—but now she really liked his

41

personality as well. *Okay*, she thought, summoning up her nerve. *Now is the moment to invite him to our party.*

"Bruce, I was wondering—" she began. But before she could get any further she spotted Miss Peabody barreling toward her. "Get rid of the chili dog!" she whispered urgently. The sight of Miss Peabody had suddenly reminded her of the "no eating" rule.

"What? Why?" he asked, confused. Impulsively Chris knocked the half-eaten dog and soda from his hand. "Chris, you just threw the lunch you gave me into the pool," Bruce pointed out, looking down at the floating cup and soggy food.

"Miss Pea—" she started to explain, but in seconds the woman was by their side.

"This is going in my report!" Miss Peabody said sharply.

"What's wrong, Miss Peabody?" Bruce asked, turning to face her.

"Ha! As if you didn't know—what is your name again?"

"Bruce Johnson."

"Why don't *you* tell me what's wrong, Johnson?"

"I don't know," he answered honestly.

"I saw you eating on the job," she said. "Not only that, you were not eating at a designated break area, nor with the permission of your supervisor." Miss Peabody's eyes widened with horror as she spotted the food floating in the pool. "And this is where you dispose of your refuse?" she asked, pointing in disgust.

"Of course not," said Bruce. "It dropped by accident."

"It was my fault," Chris spoke up. "I gave it to him and then I knocked it out of his hand."

"You're quite the little menace, aren't you, Brown?" Miss Peabody said. "I am reporting you for trying to pad your timecard."

"What?" Chris gasped.

"You heard me. You are to ask for another assignment if your previous assignment is finished. You are not to stand here lollygagging by the pool."

"I was headed that way," Chris defended herself. "I only stopped off for a second to—"

"To carry on a flirtation with this young man," Miss Peabody finished for her. "Not on company time you don't."

Chris was mortified. How dare this wretched woman humiliate her in front of Bruce like this? "I was not . . . I . . ." she sputtered.

"March up to the time clock and punch out immediately," Miss Peabody ordered her.

"But I'm on until two."

"Not today you're not," said Miss Peabody. "I can see there's a lot of fat in the system here, and it needs trimming. And we'll start right here with you."

For a moment, Chris thought Miss Peabody had called her fat. Then she realized the woman was talking about a lack of efficiency among the hotel staff. "March, Brown. The Highcourt Group is not paying you to stand around and pursue your love life."

"I was just talking to—" Chris began, red-faced with anger.

"I said march!" Miss Peabody interrupted.

Chris was so embarrassed that she couldn't even look at Bruce. As she headed for the hotel, she heard Miss Peabody continuing to scold Bruce. Angry tears welled up in Chris's eyes. "So much for being the model employee," she muttered, slamming through the door into the hotel lobby.

Chapter Seven

"You sound like you're inviting people to a funeral instead of a party," Liza scolded Chris that afternoon after work. "Lighten up a little, would you?" The girls had gone straight to Liza's house and were calling the last few friends they hadn't reached to invite them to their party.

"I can't help it," Chris grumbled. "I'm still so ticked off at that Miss Pea-Brain I could scream!"

"I think it's time for a trip to the cove," said Sam. "That always makes you feel better."

Castaway Cove was a small, sloping spot off to the left of Castaway Beach. It was almost always deserted. The girls went there—either alone or together—when they wanted to talk or think. They thought of the cove as their private retreat.

Riding through town, they passed the elegant part of Bonita Beach, with its sprawling homes hidden behind high fences and hedges. Then they turned up a dirt road and pedaled until they came to a small wooden sign with the words "Castaway Cove" burned into it. Walking their bikes through a wide, dense cluster of palm trees, they soon emerged onto the sloped, horseshoe-shaped cove.

The cool water felt good on their legs when they waded in. After swimming, they sat and talked about how rotten Miss Peabody was and then about Bruce. Sam and Liza tried desperately to convince Chris that Bruce didn't hate her because of what had happened.

"It was me who got him into trouble," said Chris. "I was the one who knocked the stupid chili dog and soda into the water."

"So, you panicked. It could happen to anyone," Sam said.

"It wouldn't happen to Jannette Sansibar," Chris sulked.

"I give up!" Liza snapped, frustrated with Chris's bad mood. "I'm sick of sitting and moping. Let's go for a walk."

"I'm not going to Castaway Beach," Chris said, burying her feet in the sand. "Bruce might be there and I can't face him."

"Oh, come on," Sam coaxed. "If he's there, we'll find out right now if he hates you or not. You won't have to sit and wonder."

"Well, maybe you're right," Chris sighed. "I suppose I might as well get it over with."

The three girls walked along the winding shoreline. It

was only six o'clock, but the beach was already taking on the bluish cast of evening.

"I think I see Lloyd, the surfer king," Sam said, pointing out to the ocean where five boys on surfboards rode the waves.

Liza peered over her shoulder. "I see Eddie with him." She turned to Chris. "Bruce is there, too."

"Forget it. I'm going back," Chris said.

"No, you're not," said Sam, dragging Chris forward by her elbow. Half wanting to run away and half wanting to know how Bruce felt, Chris let herself be dragged.

As they approached, Eddie spotted them and rode a wave close to shore. "Hi," he called, walking his board through the surf.

Liza ran into the water to meet him. "They look cute together," Sam said as Eddie put his free arm around Liza's shoulders and hugged her, and together they waded to shore.

Chris noticed Bruce coming in next. Her pulse quickened. What would he say? Would he be cool, or outright angry? Maybe he'd ignore her altogether. That would be the worst.

"Eddie's coming to the party," Liza announced happily. "Your line was busy all last night. I tried to call you," she said to Eddie.

"My sister," he explained, throwing his board onto the sand. "We call her Jaws because she never gets off the phone." He adjusted the drawstring of his colorful jams. "Is Bruce invited?"

"Of course he is," Chris jumped in eagerly. "I was

47

about to invite him today when that horrible Miss Peabody yelled at us for all this stupid stuff. It was totally my fault and I got Bruce into terrible trouble. I didn't mean to. It was an accident."

"That old bat sounds like a nightmare," said Eddie.

"Oh, she is," Chris said frantically. If Eddie understood, maybe he would take Chris's side. "She's, like, up-from-the-crypt. She has this white-white skin and horrible black hair. I just can't think straight with her breathing down my neck."

As Chris spoke, she kept one eye on Bruce as he approached them. "What are you guys talking about?" he asked.

"Miss Pea-Brain," Eddie told him.

"Oh, geez," Bruce laughed. "That was funny today, wasn't it?"

Funny? thought Chris, trying to absorb this new slant on things. *He thinks it was funny?* She was suddenly flooded with relief. "Yeah, it was pretty amusing," she bluffed.

"Man, you guys should have seen her face when she saw the food in the pool. She pointed to it like there was a dead skunk floating there." He scrunched up his face and pointed in imitation of Miss Peabody. He poked Chris playfully in the arm. "You were so cool, the way you told her, 'I was on my way back to the hotel,' with this expression like 'Don't tell me what to do.'"

"I was?" asked Chris, surprised but pleased. "I didn't feel too cool. I'm sorry I got you into trouble."

"Hey, I don't care," he chuckled. "That old ferret face isn't going to be here forever."

"She might report us to Parker though," said Chris.

"So what?" Bruce replied. "Even if he fires us, the summer is almost over. And he's not going to fire us, anyway." That was one of the many things Chris liked about Bruce. He didn't let things get to him the way she did.

The group walked to the edge of the water and sat down, letting the foamy surf wash over their legs. Chris could barely stop herself from grinning. Bruce wasn't angry with her! It was all a big joke to him. And he even thought she'd been cool.

"Here comes Wave-Master Lloyd now," quipped Chris as Lloyd surfed into shore.

"That guy is too tough," said Eddie admiringly.

"I know," Bruce agreed.

"I know you guys think he's great," said Sam. "But why?"

"For one thing, face it, the waves aren't exactly stupendous out here," said Eddie. "But Lloyd has a way of making them really work. He can get a longer ride than anybody I've ever seen."

Sam shrugged, unimpressed. "That's it?"

"No, no," said Bruce. "The guy is just . . . cool. The other day, in town, some older guys were bugging us for no reason. Lloyd just stood there like a statue, glaring at the guys until they left."

"He probably couldn't think of anything to say," Sam suggested.

"It wasn't that," Eddie insisted. "The guy has a kind of aura about him. It's hard to explain."

Sam shook her head. "You guys are crazy."

"No we're not. All the surfers know he's the king," said Bruce.

"Maybe you have to be a guy to understand Lloyd-worship," said Liza. "Maybe it's just one of those 'guy things'—you know, like finding belching funny."

"Belching *is* funny," Eddie said with a laugh.

Lloyd waded out of the water, flipping his white-blond bangs from his eyes. "Bogus waves today, man," he complained to Eddie and Bruce. "Like, totally not worth mentioning. They were really happening this morning."

"You mean you've been here all day?" cried Sam in disbelief.

"All day every day," Lloyd answered.

"The man is devoted," Eddie said enthusiastically.

"Hey, you guys going to the shindig these girls are throwing?" Lloyd asked.

Bruce looked surprised. "I was about to invite you when Pea-Brain jumped all over us," Chris explained. "It's this Saturday."

"Sure. I'll be there," Bruce replied.

Yes! Yes! Chris thought triumphantly. She'd gone from the pits of depression to complete joy. Now she and Bruce had a new bond between them. They were partners in crime. It was something they could laugh about together. In September, in school, she could wave to him and say, "What's that floating in the pool, young man?"

He'd laugh, and everyone would know they shared a private joke.

And now he was coming to the party. She'd have to think of lots of witty things to say about Miss Peabody. If she could keep him entertained, maybe she'd get an edge on Jannette. Just then, who should come walking across the beach with a group of other kids but . . . Jannette, wearing a flowered bikini that showed off her slim figure. She put down her blanket with the others, but looked at Bruce. "Hey, Jannette," he called to her.

Just when things were going so well, too, Chris thought dejectedly. As she watched Jannette approach, looking trim and terrific in her colorful suit, Chris suddenly felt as though she weighed two hundred pounds. Her good spirits faded as she looked at the expression on Bruce's face. He'd gotten up off his elbows and was now watching Jannette's every move.

Sickening, thought Chris sullenly.

"You all look like you're having a nice friendly chat," said Jannette, coming up beside them. "Anything interesting?"

"We're talking about Miss Peabody," Bruce told her. He'd stood up—and was a little too close to Jannette for Chris's taste.

"She seems like a dear," cooed Jannette.

"A dear!" cried Sam. "She's a horror show."

Jannette delicately smoothed back her silky blond hair. "I didn't have any difficulty with her," she said.

"Jannette gets along with everyone," Bruce said,

admiration filling his voice. "She sees the good in everybody."

Bruce's words hit Chris in the stomach. Was he really so blind that he couldn't tell what a phony she was? If Jannette got along with people, it was because she barely noticed them. Jannette was the only person who interested Jannette. Except Bruce. Apparently he interested Jannette quite a bit.

"You must be Lloyd Kramer," Jannette said to Lloyd.

"How did you know?" asked Lloyd, clearly flattered.

"Bruce tells me what a great surfer you are," Jannette replied. "He says you're the king."

Lloyd shuffled with pleasant embarrassment. "Gee, I didn't know I was famous."

"You are so adorable." Jannette laughed flirtatiously. "You're practically a legend in Bonita Beach."

"I'm going to puke," Sam whispered to Chris.

Chris nodded, rolling her eyes. Lloyd's next words caught her completely by surprise.

"You're coming to the big bash on Saturday, aren't you?" said Lloyd. "Sammy and the girls are throwing a shindig."

"A party!" Jannette said, smiling. "I adore parties."

Chapter Eight

On Thursday morning, Mrs. Chan was still out sick. As Miss Peabody stood next to the front desk reading off the day's assignments, Liza, Chris and Sam stood behind Sunny, Lillian and Jannette. "Why can't she just tack it on the board and shut up, already?" Liza whispered to Chris.

"Because she loves to hear herself talk," Chris whispered back.

"Shhh, she's looking right at you," Sam warned.

The warning came too late. "Brown, could you possibly wait until I'm finished?" Miss Peabody snapped. "I have to say that I'm shocked Mr. Parker tolerates such disrespectful attitudes from some of his staff."

"Sorry," Chris muttered. She had never disliked anyone as much as she disliked this woman—not even Mr. Parker.

"Velez, you will be playing checkers with Mr. Hyram Schwartz," Miss Peabody read. "For some reason Mr.

Schwartz requested you. Let me remind you that he is a long-term guest and is to be treated with the utmost respect."

"I know Mr. Schwartz," Liza cut in. "He and I are friends."

Miss Peabody's nostrils flared. "Yes, well, you are not here to befriend the guests. You are here to serve them. Understood?"

Liza stood silently seething as Miss Peabody continued. "O'Neill, you will be caring for Mercy Evans, age two. And Brown, you are to pick up the Wanamaker twins. I've given you twins since you seemed to have so much extra time on your hands the other day. But let me warn you, Mr. Wanamaker is a multimillionaire. He has two suites on the seventeenth floor. You watch those children like a hawk, and treat them with kid gloves. Do I make myself clear?"

"I always try to do a good job," Chris replied.

"See that you do one today," Miss Peabody snapped. "You have your assignments," she concluded and walked off.

"She is the most horrendous creature in the whole universe," Sam spoke first.

"I'd like to pop her one in the nose," said the short redhead named Sunny. "She made me wipe off my eyeliner right out by the pool yesterday. I looked like a raccoon all morning."

"I know, and she jumped down my throat just for giving a little boy an ice pop," added Lillian.

"Miss Peabody has a responsibility to her company," Jannette said. "She's only doing her job."

"Don't you think she's a teensy bit on the nasty side, Jannette?" Liza pointed out irritably. "Not to mention completely humorless and unreasonable."

"She is the boss," Jannette reminded Liza needlessly. "Oh, and I'm looking forward to the party Saturday."

Sam, Chris and Liza exchanged glances. They knew they were stuck with Jannette. If they un-invited her, they'd have to explain why. And that wouldn't go over well with Bruce at all.

"Yeah, it'll be fun," Sam mumbled.

A skinny, deeply wrinkled old man dressed in a baggy, light blue summer suit hobbled into the lobby leaning on his cane. "Here comes Chas now," Liza said, calling Mr. Schwartz by his former stage name, which had been Chas Reynolds. From the moment he revealed he'd once been a stunt double and an actor, Mr. Schwartz had become Chas to Liza. "Time to go lose at checkers," she said merrily as she ran off to meet him.

"I guess she's mine," said Sam, nodding toward a two-year-old walking into the lobby with her mother.

After a few moments, two seven-year-old twin girls wearing identical blue bathing suits and carrying beach bags came into the lobby with their mother. With their tight red curls, dark brown eyes and button noses, the girls looked like twin Raggedy Ann dolls come to life. They were pint-sized versions of their mother, who wore a denim shift with large red patch pockets. Chris would never have guessed Mrs. Wanamaker was even rich enough to stay at the Palm—let alone take up two luxury suites.

"Mrs. Wanamaker, I'm Chris Brown, your baby sitter," Chris said as she approached the woman.

"Why hi there, gal," Mrs. Wanamaker spoke with a hearty Texas twang. "Meet Dolly and Tammy."

"I'm Dolly."

"I'm Tammy." The girls spoke at once.

"Chrissy here can take you to the beach if you promise to be real good," Mrs. Wanamaker said to her daughters.

"All right," they answered at once. The girls hugged their mother and, at the exact same moment, planted kisses on either side of her cheek. Then they turned and grinned at Chris. She noticed they were both missing one front tooth. *Dolly's left tooth is out, and Tammy's right tooth is missing*, she noted. *Thank goodness*, thought Chris. *Now I'll know who's who.*

Chris led them through the lobby, out past the pools and down to the beach. The twins said nothing the whole way, but giggled shyly and whispered to each other.

They're cute, thought Chris as the twins pulled their identical blankets from their bags and set them down. Tammy pulled out a coloring book and the two girls set to neatly working on the same picture of a cowgirl on a pony. *I got lucky today*, thought Chris, leaning back on her chair. *These two are good kids.*

Chris gazed out lazily onto the beach. There were only four other people on it, since it was not yet even nine-thirty. The sun danced on the water and a soft breeze ruffled the palm trees.

She was glad to have some time to think. She had to come up with a way of keeping Bruce's attention at the party, even though Jannette would be there. *I could ask him to help me make something,* she plotted. Yes, that was it. She'd put out a vegetable dip and then pretend to run out of cut veggies. Bruce was a nice guy. He'd help her chop carrots and celery if she asked him.

Pleased with this idea, Chris began to daydream about how it would go. Maybe he'd accidentally nick his finger and she'd help him bandage it. Then, while she was close to him, he'd sweep her into his arms and kiss her. . . .

"Why are you smiling?" Tammy's voice roused Chris.

"Ummm . . . I was thinking about a friend who I like a lot," Chris answered.

"That's nice," Dolly said wistfully. "Tammy and I miss our friends back in Dallas."

Something in Dolly's sad smile touched Chris. She remembered taking vacations with her family when she was younger. Even a week away from Sam and Liza had seemed like a long time. She tried to think of something that would make Dolly feel better. "I have an idea," said Chris. "Why don't we make cards to send to your friends?"

Tammy and Dolly looked perplexed. "What will we use for envelopes?"

Chris dug through her bag and pulled out a white pad she carried. "We can draw pictures and then fold the paper over and tape it shut," she explained.

The little girls still looked doubtful. "Here, I'll show you," said Chris, picking up a black crayon from the pile

Tammy had left scattered on her coloring book. She drew stick figures of two girls. Then, using an orange crayon, she drew a tousle of curls on each figure's head. She finished the sketch with the blue sea and sky, a tall palm and a smiling sun. In red crayon, she wrote the words, "Having a great time!" Then she held it up.

"Hey! That's us!" Tammy cried gleefully.

"At the beach!" added Dolly. "Can we send that one to my friend Alice?"

"Sure," said Chris, handing her the card. "Sign it, and then we can get a stamp and some tape at the front desk when we go in."

"This is neat," said Dolly.

Chris tore off a sheet of paper for each of them. "Now you make your own cards," she said. Tammy and Dolly began drawing immediately, giggling as they stole peeks at each other's work.

They spent the next hour drawing and laughing over their pictures. Before she'd started baby-sitting, Chris had never realized how much she liked kids. But she did like them, and she thought Dolly and Tammy were especially sweet.

"Ices. Homemade strawberry ices!" Chris looked up and saw a man walking up the beach carrying a cooler. Peddlers weren't allowed on the hotel beach, but that didn't stop them from trying. People were always selling food, candy and coral jewelry until someone from the hotel came down and chased them.

"Want ices?" Chris asked Tammy and Dolly.

"Yeah!" they shouted together.

Chris called the man over and asked for three ices. Then remembering her diet, she changed it to two ices. "Have three," the man coaxed. "I made them myself, from real strawberries."

"Two is enough." Chris smiled, fishing money from her shorts pocket. She noticed Tammy and Dolly urgently whispering back and forth. Tammy was shaking her head no, while Dolly nodded yes. "Is something the matter?" Chris asked.

The girls shook their heads. "You're sure?" Chris pressed, unconvinced. The girls nodded vigorously in unison. Chris handed them the ices and went back to her romantic daydreams of Bruce.

After they finished the ices, Dolly asked if they could go into the water. "Sure," Chris said as she got up to take them. She stood up to her knees in the surf while they played together, splashing and blowing bubbles. They were dunking each other when suddenly Tammy cried out and pointed at Dolly's face.

When she reached the girl, Chris immediately saw two large red welts on Dolly's forehead and one on her cheek. "I told her not to eat the strawberries!" cried Tammy. "She's allergic."

"That was strawberry ice. It doesn't count," replied Dolly, touching the bumps with her hands.

"I guess it does count," observed Chris. "How do you feel?"

"Itchy," Dolly admitted. She began scratching her arm and Chris noticed two more hives near her elbow.

"Are you also allergic?" Chris asked Tammy.

"Nope," Tammy answered, shaking her head.

"Thank goodness. What does your mom do when this happens?" Chris asked, trying not to panic.

"I don't know," said Tammy. "Nothing really."

"Come on," said Chris, "we'd better try to find your mother or father." She put her arm around Dolly's shoulder and ushered her out of the water. *She doesn't seem to be in pain or anything*, Chris thought, *but I'd better not take any chances.*

Quickly gathering up their things, Chris hurried the two girls up to the hotel. She sighed when she saw Miss Peabody behind the front desk. She didn't look forward to telling the woman her problem. Somehow she was sure Miss Peabody would find a way to blame her. *I guess I don't have any choice*, she told herself.

Dolly and Tammy clutched their towels around their shivering shoulders as they walked into the air conditioning. They followed Chris to the front desk. "How are you doing?" Chris asked Dolly.

"She's itchy," said Tammy.

"Still itchy," Dolly confirmed.

Chris caught Miss Peabody's eye. "Do you know if the Wanamakers are still at the hotel?" she asked.

"I believe I saw them leave. Is there a problem?" Eyeing Chris suspiciously, Miss Peabody leaned over the desk ledge. Before Chris was even able to answer, Miss Peabody noticed Dolly. "What's happened to her face?" she cried.

"She's had an allergic reaction to—" Chris began.

"Oh, my heavens!" Miss Peabody gasped, cutting her off. "What will we do?"

"I thought if we could get in touch with her parents, they'd know—"

"No time," Miss Peabody cried shuffling frantically through papers on the desk. "Where is that number? I just saw it," she muttered. "Ah, here it is!" She began punching numbers into the phone.

"What are you—" Chris ventured.

"Hello, Emergency Services?" Miss Peabody spoke into the receiver. "This is the Palm Pavilion. We have a sick child. Yes. Severe allergic reaction. Horrible welts all over the face and body." Miss Peabody covered the phone and asked Chris, "Any other symptoms?"

"No," Chris answered.

"Throat closing over. Trouble breathing. Losing consciousness. You must hurry."

Miss Peabody put down the receiver with a bang and came flying out from behind the desk. "Miss Peabody, I don't think she's really that bad," Chris told her.

"Those people take their time unless you exaggerate," said Miss Peabody. "And this hotel will not be sued by the Wanamakers. Not while I'm in charge." As she spoke, Miss Peabody scooped up Dolly, who was now wide-eyed with surprise, and carried her off toward the front entrance.

Chris took Tammy's hand and tried to keep up with the bustling woman. "Is Dolly going to die?" Tammy asked Chris, panicking.

"No, no, of course not," Chris told her, still trying to

keep pace with Miss Peabody. Chris heard the sound of a siren. *That must be the ambulance coming*, she realized.

Then another, much louder noise began approaching with ever-increasing volume. *Thwap! Thwap! Thwap!*

"What's that?" asked Tammy.

Chris stood and listened. "It sounds like a helicopter."

Chapter Nine

The sound of the helicopter was almost deafening as it landed on the sprawling golf course. Chris stood behind Miss Peabody at the front entrance and watched a tall, balding man jump out and run toward the hotel. At the same time, the ambulance zoomed up the front drive, its siren blaring.

Dolly stood with Miss Peabody, clutching her towel around her shoulders, her skinny legs quaking. Chris held Tammy's hand. "How do you feel?" she asked Dolly.

"Itchy," Dolly replied. "Are they going to take me away?"

Chris looked around anxiously. It certainly appeared as if they were going to take Dolly—one way or another. "They just want to make sure you're all right," she replied.

Tammy threw her arms around her twin. "Don't let them take my sister!" she screamed.

"I don't want to go!" Dolly cried at the same time.

"Quiet!" Miss Peabody spoke sharply. "You're a very sick girl."

"I'm not sick!"

"She's not sick!"

The medics from the ambulance, a short blond woman and a stocky man with a beard, were right behind the medic from the helicopter. "We're here for a sick child," the helicopter medic addressed Miss Peabody.

"Here she is," Miss Peabody said, gently pushing Dolly forward.

The helicopter medic knelt in front of Dolly. "What hurts, hon?" he asked kindly.

"I itch."

"She itches," Tammy joined in.

The man looked up at Miss Peabody. "Is that it?" he inquired, perplexed.

"What do you mean, is that it?" Miss Peabody replied anxiously. "Look at the child. She's covered with welts."

The blond medic knelt beside the man from the helicopter. "You mean these little pink marks?"

Chris realized that the hives were subsiding. Dolly now looked as if she had several oversize mosquito bites on her face and arms. "She said her throat felt funny," Miss Peabody volunteered.

The blond woman took a penlight and looked down Dolly's throat. "It's a little red," she said. "In a severe allergic reaction the throat can close up. That's why we take it seriously. But she looks okay to me. No danger."

All the while, Tammy had kept her hand protectively on Dolly's shoulder. "She'll be okay," Chris whispered to

Tammy. She was glad Dolly wasn't seriously ill, but she was beginning to feel foolish that all this commotion had been caused over a few spots.

"We can probably handle her at General," said the stocky medic. "I don't think you have to fly her to Downstate."

"Downstate has a better pediatric," the helicopter medic pointed out. "Let's take her just to be safe."

The three medics placed Dolly on a stretcher and strapped her in.

"I need an accompanying adult," the helicopter medic said.

"All right," said Miss Peabody. "I suppose that's me."

"I don't want to go!" screamed Dolly, terrified.

"You'll be fine," said Chris reassuringly.

"This is all your fault, Brown," said Miss Peabody. "You should have checked for allergies."

"My fault!" cried Chris. "I didn't know!"

Before they could argue any further, the medics carried Dolly toward the helicopter. Miss Peabody followed them, casting a worried glance back at the hotel.

Just then Mrs. Wanamaker came rushing up the drive. "What is going on?" she asked Chris in a panicked voice. "Where are they taking my baby?"

"She's okay," Chris told her. "But she had a strawberry ice and she broke out in hives. They're flying her to the hospital."

"Oh, good gracious!" Mrs. Wanamaker cried, running

toward the helicopter. Tammy broke free of Chris's hand and followed her mother.

What a mess, thought Chris, chasing Tammy. *And all for a few hives*. The helicopter was once again starting its engines. Chris's hair blew wildly around her head as the vehicle's blades began to whirl.

Chris saw Mrs. Wanamaker catch up with Dolly, just as they lifted her into the copter. "Are you the mother?" the medic shouted, trying to be heard above the helicopter.

"Sure am," Mrs. Wanamaker shouted back. "Is this really necessary? The symptoms will go away so long as she quits eating those darned berries."

"Sorry," yelled the helicopter medic. "We have to make a thorough check and file a report. Would you like to accompany us in the helicopter?"

Mrs. Wanamaker sighed with annoyance. "My husband was going to take the twins fishing this afternoon. Oh, well."

"I don't want to go in the helicopter!" yelled Dolly, clutching Tammy, who was now beside her. "I'm afraid. I'm afraid."

"I appreciate your concern," Mrs. Wanamaker said to Miss Peabody. "But couldn't you have just taken her to the doctor or something?"

"I agree," shouted Miss Peabody. "I told that to Christine, but she'd already dialed emergency. You know how overly dramatic teenagers are."

Chris's jaw dropped in shock.

"You did your best, I guess," said Mrs. Wanamaker,

climbing into the helicopter and pulling Tammy up after her. "But this is a darned inconvenience. We only have one more day of vacation, and now we'll be spending it in a hospital."

"We're ready," the copter pilot called. "Clear the field."

"Tell Mr. Wanamaker what happened!" called Mrs. Wanamaker as Chris and Miss Peabody backed away from the helicopter. In a minute, the copter lifted off the ground and Chris and Miss Peabody ran back to the hotel.

A large man wearing a straw cowboy hat stopped Miss Peabody. "You haven't seen my wife, have you, Miss Peabody?" he asked. "I was parking the car and she seems to have disappeared on me."

Miss Peabody smiled nervously as she explained that his wife and children were in the helicopter directly overhead. "Christine here just completely overreacted," she told the man. "On behalf of the hotel, I sincerely apologize."

"Give me directions to this Downstate place," he said, annoyed. "That little allergy isn't worth all this fuss."

"Apologize to Mr. Wanamaker, Christine," said Miss Peabody.

This was too much. Miss Peabody was pushing Chris to the limits of her patience. How much could she take? "I'm sorry I gave her the ice, sir," Chris spoke, "but Miss Peabody here is the one who decided to call Emergency Services."

67

"Christine, you don't need to cover up," said Miss Peabody. "It's very unattractive."

"I don't believe you!" cried Chris. "You're lying. Maybe you did the right thing by calling emergency. I don't know. But you're the one who did it."

"Christine, I won't tolerate this defiance," said Miss Peabody angrily. "I have a good mind to fire you."

Chris was furious with this ridiculous, cowardly woman. "You can't fire me!" Chris cried out. "I can't stand working for you one more day. I quit!"

Chapter Ten

Sam, Liza and Chris sat at Chris's kitchen table. "Let's put these away right now," said Liza, shoving the box of chocolate-chip cookies to the corner of the table. "We've had enough. And I use the term 'we' very loosely," she added, staring at Chris.

"I need them," said Chris, pulling the box back to her. "I'm too aggravated to stop eating."

Sam wiped a milk mustache from her upper lip. "I can't believe Pea-Brain tried to blame you for what she did."

Liza grabbed the cookie box and covered it with her arms. "Okay, so that's no reason to blow your diet. The party is only two days away. You might still lose a few pounds if you don't go crazy and try to eat away your problems."

Chris reached across the table and attempted to pry the box out from under Liza's arms. "What are you, my diet counselor? Give me those cookies. Now!"

"It's this kind of emotional connection to food that is going to keep you a pudgette for the rest of your life," Liza insisted.

"For Pete's sake, give her the cookies, Liza," said Sam. "Can't you see she's having a bad day?"

Liza slid the box to Chris. "Don't blame me when they start calling you Blimpo Brown."

"Ha, ha," mumbled Chris, chomping on a cookie. "It's not every day a person quits a job. I'm entitled to be upset. And when I'm upset, I eat cookies. Okay?"

"We'll be back to school in a week," Liza said consolingly. "So what's the big deal?"

"You guys were planning to quit the Palm when school starts?" Chris asked, surprised.

"No, not really," Sam admitted. "But we won't be able to work as much. We might make less than half of what we're making now."

"Maybe I should have just apologized to the guy and kept my mouth shut," Chris considered gloomily. "At least then I'd still have a job."

"Oh, how could you have not said something to that witch!" cried Sam. "You'd be a total wimp if you let her dump on you like that and didn't say a word."

"I'd be a wimp with a job," Chris sulked. "And now I have no chance with Bruce."

"What are you talking about?" cried Liza. "He'll be at the party and you'll see him at school."

"Yeah, and Jannette will be at the party. Then once we're in school, he'll be a junior and we'll be dumb freshmen. He won't want to know us," Chris argued.

"Bruce isn't like that," said Sam.

"Maybe not. Who knows?" said Chris, digging into the cookie box. All she knew was that she wanted to punch Miss Peabody. Adults—even awful ones like Miss Peabody—weren't supposed to go around lying like that. She expected adults to be a pain in the neck sometimes. They could be thick-headed, irrational and overbearing. But she could not accept being blamed for something an adult had done. "Why would she do something like that?" Chris asked for the twentieth time since that afternoon.

"Because she didn't want Mr. Wanamaker to blame her," said Liza, tilting her chair back.

"But so what?" said Chris. "What could he do to her?"

"Sue the hotel," Sam suggested.

"For what? Overenthusiasm in protecting his child's health?" said Chris.

"Face it, Chris," Liza said. "She simply didn't want to take the blame for freaking out in a crisis. I don't know why you think that grownups don't do the same crummy things that kids do."

"I guess," said Chris. "But what's the point of getting older if you don't get smarter and better at dealing with things?"

"Not everybody is like Miss Peabody," Sam reminded her. "But I know what you mean. Sometimes people really make you embarrassed to be human."

"That's for sure," Chris agreed glumly. "I wish I were a dolphin, then I'd just swim around and eat squid all day."

"Hey, even dolphins have bad days," said Liza. "Look at that one who was so sweet. He got clobbered by that boat."

"Poor dolphin," Chris muttered. "I hope he's okay."

"Me, too," said Sam, pushing her chair back. "My father says that one of the boat captains reported seeing a dolphin swimming by himself, and he looked slow and wobbly."

"Oh, man, that's sad," sighed Liza.

"Yeah," Sam agreed. "I've got to get going. It's Trevor's birthday, so Lloyd and Greta are cooking a special dinner."

"Don't tell me they're making a Chompy Pet casserole," groaned Liza.

"No, I think they're actually grilling steaks, but with Lloyd around, you never know," Sam answered. "See ya."

Liza and Chris walked Sam to the door, then they flopped down on the bed in Chris's room. "Is there anything I should do for the party since I now have tons of time on my hands?" Chris asked.

Liza thought. "If you have money, you could shop for pretzels and stuff like that," she suggested.

"Okay," Chris agreed. The two girls began thumbing through some fashion and beauty magazines that were scattered on the floor. All the models were slim, most of them were blond. They all seemed so beautiful and energetic—just like Jannette. What did Chris have to offer that could compete with that? *Nothing that I can think of*, she admitted.

"Liza," Chris asked seriously. "Do you think I should give up on Bruce?"

"Why?" Liza asked, looking up from her magazine.

"You know why," Chris insisted. "Bruce is blond and gorgeous. Jannette is blond and gorgeous. Maybe they belong together."

Liza considered this. "Maybe they do," she said with a shrug.

"Liza!" Chris cried. "That's not what you're supposed to say!"

"Well, do you want them to belong together?" Liza asked. "You sound as if you've already given up. I did see you eat almost a whole box of cookies just now, didn't I?"

"I know," admitted Chris, tossing her magazines across the room in disgust. "It's just that Jannette is so . . . so *perfect*. I don't have a chance against her."

Liza looked at Chris. "Let's be honest. None of us is Jannette in the looks department. But you're cute, Chris. Maybe with a perm or something you'd look more glamorous. Bruce probably thinks of you as a buddy, and not a *real* girl."

Chris went to her full-length mirror. "Do you think I'd look good as a blond?" she asked.

"You are blond," noted Liza.

"You know what I mean, a blond like Jannette." Chris sucked in her round cheeks and tried to picture herself with flowing white-blond tresses. It would certainly change her image.

"I don't know," said Liza skeptically. "It's not really you."

73

"That's the point, though!" cried Chris. "Really me doesn't get Bruce's attention. A blond might be more appealing." She wondered how she'd feel as a light blond.

"You'd always be touching up the roots," Liza pointed out. "Not to mention that your mother would kill you."

"True," said Chris. "But once it was done, there'd be nothing she could do about it."

Chapter Eleven

On Friday morning when Chris woke up, it felt strange not to have to dress for work. She threw a robe over the T-shirt she always wore to bed and trudged sleepily into the kitchen.

Her mother was already at the table, drinking coffee. "I was sure you'd sleep late this morning," she said as Chris sat down.

"I couldn't sleep," Chris yawned. "I'm too used to getting up early."

Mrs. Brown smiled. "This won't be so bad. You'll be back to school soon. And today is the last day of summer school. I'll be home and we can do things together."

"That will be nice," Chris said politely. Hanging out with her mother for the rest of the summer wasn't her idea of fun, but she knew her mother was just trying to help.

"What will you do with your day off?" Mrs. Brown asked, carrying her coffee into the living room with her.

"I'm going to shop for our party," Chris said. After she went shopping she planned to come home and bleach her hair. She knew doing it without her mother's permission was risky. If her mother got angry enough, she might ground her and keep her from going to the party. "Mom . . . I thought I might do something with my hair," Chris ventured cautiously.

Her mother raised one eyebrow. "Like what?" she asked suspiciously.

"Ummm . . . like bleach it blond," Chris answered as casually as she could.

"You have beautiful strawberry-blond hair," her mother protested. "Why would you want to change it?"

"I know but it's so . . . ordinary. I just want to lighten it a little."

"How little?"

Good, thought Chris. *She's weakening.* "So it looks like I spent the summer outside in the sun," she answered.

"You did spend the summer outside in the sun," her mother reminded her.

"Come on, Mom," Chris begged. "I look so blah. It's my hair."

"Streaks," her mother relented. "A few light streaks in the front. That's it."

Better than nothing, thought Chris. "Okay, streaks, just a few streaks."

"All right," her mother agreed, heading for the front door.

"Just streaks," Chris said, springing off the couch.

Now she was excited! She dressed quickly and took her baby-sitting money out of her top dresser drawer.

As she rode her bike into town, she tried to envision herself with glamorous streaks in her hair. Yes, it was just the touch of sex appeal that she needed. She pulled up in front of Myer's Supermarket, where she picked up the food they needed for the party.

Her last stop was the beauty aisle, where she carefully chose a hair-streaking kit.

Chris was home by noon. Her father had left, and the house was quiet. She opened her hair kit in the bathroom. There were white tubes and vials, plastic gloves, a sheet of instructions and a wide plastic cap with small holes in it.

Tying on the plastic bonnet, she began pulling hair through the holes with a small curved hook that had come in the kit. *No one will even notice the difference,* she decided after pulling hair up in the front. A few more strands wouldn't hurt. The movement became almost hypnotic as she worked along the side and down the back of her head. Her arms tired when she reached the back and she decided it was enough. *Maybe I've kind of overdone it,* she worried. But she wasn't about to take the whole bonnet off and start again—not after all that work. *These are just streaks*, she reminded herself. *My other hair will cover it.*

Her next step was to mix up the bleach and smear it on the hair she'd pulled out of the bonnet. After wrapping it in a plastic cover, she checked her watch. It was twelve-thirty. She'd check her hair at ten minutes before one.

In her room, Chris pulled out the black dress she'd decided to wear to the party. It was loose and short, and, most importantly, black. Black always made her look thinner. She was going to look great in the black dress with her blond-streaked hair.

Sorting through the jewelry in her top drawer, Chris decided to wear her large red hoop earrings. *Perfect with the black dress and blond hair,* she thought. Her look was really coming together.

At ten to one she returned to the bathroom and checked her hair. The strand she wiped clean was a lemony yellow. *Any blonder and it will be white,* she thought, trying not to panic. She stuck her head under the shower and washed off the rest of the bleach. Anxiously, she pulled off the cap. The streaks stood up in clumps away from her natural reddish blond hair.

Okay, stay calm, she told herself. *After it's washed and blown, it will all blend together.* Chris ran back to her room and blew out her hair.

When it was done she gazed at her reflection in the mirror. It was a little startling—but she loved it. She loved the way it brought out the green in her hazel eyes, and the way it flowed softly around her face. It was beautiful!

Then she remembered her mother's words: "Just a few streaks." This was quite a bit more than a few streaks.

"What if she grounds me?" Chris worried out loud. "If I don't go to the party, I won't see Bruce again until

78

school." She'd have to find a way to conceal her hair until the party was over. After that, she'd face her mother and take the consequences.

It was almost two o'clock. Sam and Liza would be home soon. She'd go to Sam's and wait. Mrs. O'Neill wouldn't mind.

Quickly gathering some toiletries, a nightshirt and the clothing she'd be wearing at the party, Chris put it all in her old school knapsack. Then she grabbed some paper and a pencil from the kitchen table. "I've gone to Sam's to work on the party," she wrote. "I may sleep over. I'll call you. Love, Chris." *I'm sleeping over at your house whether you want me to or not, Sam,* thought Chris as she hurried out the front door.

Chapter Twelve

"You look so cool," Liza said to Chris. It was Saturday evening and the girls were setting out bowls of chips and pretzels on the picnic table in Sam's yard.

Chris was already dressed for the party. Staying over at Sam's had definitely been a smart move. Chris had been able to get ready for the party without worrying about her mother seeing her hair, and now she felt as though she'd never looked better. She'd set her hair in instant rollers, so she had soft, bouncy curls. And Liza—who was handy with makeup—had done Chris's face, applying more eye makeup than she usually wore. "I feel like somebody else," Chris said excitedly.

"But is that good?" asked Sam as she hung paper Japanese lanterns from the trees in her yard.

"Sure it's good," said Chris. "The old me wasn't getting anywhere with Bruce."

"I suppose," Sam said, sounding doubtful.

"I don't look radically different, do I?" Chris asked

nervously as she carried her vegetable platter into the yard.

"No," Liza assured her. "You just look more foxy, that's all."

At seven, guests started arriving, and Sam popped a tape into her portable stereo box.

"Hey, cool bash," said Lloyd, coming into the yard with an armful of tapes and Greta by his side. Mrs. O'Neill had asked Lloyd and Greta to chaperone the party. Greta had grumbled, but Lloyd was always ready for a party. "I brought some of my favorites," he told Sam, dumping the tapes into her arms.

"Beach Boys, Beach Boys and more Beach Boys," Sam said, looking through the tapes.

"You can't go wrong with the Beach Boys," Lloyd commented confidently.

"No, I guess not," said Sam, piling the tapes on the ground next to the box. "Thanks."

Chris greeted her friends, most of whom she knew from the neighborhood and school. The girls all complimented her for looking terrific, though some of them weren't sure what she'd changed. She kept looking for Bruce, anxiously waiting for his arrival.

Finally she saw Liza standing with Eddie. Liza noticed her and nodded toward the house. There stood Bruce talking with Lloyd.

Chris excused herself from the group she was talking to and made a beeline for Bruce. "Hi," she said, smiling.

"Great party," he said. "Hey, I heard what happened with Peabody. What a drag." His eyes narrowed a moment, as though he were trying to figure out why she looked different.

"Chrissy's pretty gutsy," said Lloyd as he gulped down a can of soda.

Thank you, Lloyd. Thank you, thought Chris. If Lloyd said it, Bruce would believe it. "I couldn't let her push me around," said Chris, trying to sound casual.

The three of them continued to talk about Miss Peabody and how awful she was. Chris was grateful to Lloyd. He knew she liked Bruce, and he kept saying complimentary things about her. From time to time she checked on her plate of veggies. No one was eating them. Few as there were, they were all still sitting there, untouched.

Oh, well, she thought, seeing that Jannette hadn't arrived yet. *Maybe I won't even need them.* Things were going better than she'd expected.

At eight o'clock a dusky glow fell over the yard. Sam turned on the colored lanterns and the yard took on a festive, almost magical look. Someone had put on one of Lloyd's Beach Boys tapes, and a group of kids had started dancing.

"See," said Lloyd, "those tapes do it every time."

"Want to dance?" Chris asked Bruce, feeling happily confident.

"Sure," he answered.

They joined the group of kids who were dancing. Bruce smiled at her as he began to move to the music, and she returned his smile.

Another fast song came on and they continued dancing. *I wonder what will happen when a slow song comes on*, thought Chris. Maybe he'd take her in his arms and they'd sway to the music there under the gentle light from the lanterns.

Just as Chris was thinking this, she noticed that Bruce was looking over her shoulder. She turned and there was Jannette, talking with another girl. Chris had never seen Jannette look so gorgeous. She had on a sleek, shiny cobalt-blue pantsuit. A wide, white belt showed off her tiny waist, and her hair was braided to one side. She looked like a magazine cover model.

"This is a great album, isn't it?" Chris said, trying to regain Bruce's attention.

"Huh? Oh, yeah. It is," he said distractedly. They danced until the end of the song and then a slow tune came on. "That was fun," said Bruce, indicating that he no longer wanted to dance. "I'm going to go get a soda."

"Okay," said Chris, trying to hide her disappointment.

"Do you want one?" he asked. Something in his tone told her he was only being polite, but she didn't care.

"Sure," she answered brightly. He ran off and soon returned with a can of soda.

"Here you go," he said, popping it open for her. They drank for a moment without talking. Chris could see Bruce following Jannette's every move as she circulated among the other guests. Finally, Jannette made her way over to where they stood.

"Hi there," she said in her flirtatious singsong voice. "This is a super party, Chris."

"Thanks," Chris replied. She couldn't stand the way

Bruce had changed when Jannette approached. He was standing up completely straight, his chin raised, attentive to every word she uttered. It seemed to Chris that he wasn't himself at all.

"You changed your hair," Jannette noted.

"Ummm . . . yeah," said Chris.

"I knew you looked different," Bruce said.

Jannette tossed her braid. "I'm lucky to have naturally blond hair. I don't have to bother with all that bleach. You'd better be careful, Chrissy. That stuff destroys your hair. You'll be bald if you overdo it."

"Don't worry about it, Jannette. All right?" Chris snapped.

"I was only saying—" Jannette began.

"I have to go check on the food," Chris cut her off. She had to get out of there. There was no way she could stand watching Bruce gaze at Jannette with love-stricken eyes. And she'd been making such good progress with him, too!

Liza met her halfway to the picnic table. "What are you, crazy? Get back there!" she ordered. "Why are you letting Jannette have him all to herself?"

"He doesn't know I'm alive when she's around," Chris complained.

"He danced with you, didn't he?" Sam said, joining them. "What about that vegetable dish plan you had?"

"The plate is full," Chris said, pointing at the plate on the picnic table.

"Come here," said Liza, pulling Chris to the table. She picked up the veggie plate and walked over to a tree.

84

With a quick motion she dumped the vegetables onto the ground behind it. "There, now the plate is empty," she said, presenting Chris with the plate.

"That's so wasteful!" Chris objected.

"Trevor will eat it," said Sam, who had followed them. "Go ask Bruce to help you."

Chris clutched the plate. Bruce and Jannette were still together, and Jannette was laughing at something he'd said.

"Bruce, could you give me a hand?" Chris practiced as she approached. "Bruce, can I borrow you for a moment? I need an eensy favor, Bruce." When she reached them they were so engrossed in conversation that they didn't even notice her. "Bruce," she began in a small voice. The boy looked up at her as if he'd been roused from a delightful dream. "These . . . ummm . . . these vegetables . . ." Chris stammered. "If you wouldn't mind—"

"Oh, I simply adore this song," Jannette interrupted. "You have to dance with me, Bruce. You just have to."

Bruce looked at Chris. "I'll be right back," he said as Jannette dragged him away to the grass.

Chris leaned against a tree, holding the empty plate. She waited until the end of the song. But then another one came on and Bruce kept dancing with Jannette. Finally a slow song came on and Jannette slipped into Bruce's arms, laying her head on his shoulder.

All of a sudden, hot tears filled Chris's eyes. She couldn't bear to watch Bruce and Jannette for another second. She suddenly felt ridiculous with her bleached hair and empty plate. *I have to get out of here,* she thought.

She noticed Sam and Liza coming toward her. She didn't want to talk to them because then she'd really start to cry. Blinded by tears, she dropped the plate and ran toward the house.

"Are you okay?" asked Sam as Chris rushed by.

"I just want to be alone, okay?" she said in a choked voice. Then she ran inside and straight to Sam's room, where she took off her dress and threw it on the floor. Wiping away her tears, she put on the shorts and T-shirt she'd been wearing the day before and ran out of the house.

Desperate to escape, Chris found her bike, which was leaning against Sam's garage. Not sure where she intended to go, she got on the bike and rode down Sam's driveway, away from the party.

Chapter Thirteen

Chris turned right, then left, without thinking, as if the bike had a mind of its own. Soon, though, she realized that the bumpy, moonlit dirt road before her led to Castaway Cove.

It was a cloudless night, clear and crisp, with a soft breeze ruffling the foliage. In the distance she could hear the crashing waves. Even without the moonlight, she would have known where to turn in for the cove. As she walked her bike through the cluster of palms, the darkness frightened her for the first time. But by following the ocean sounds she was able to find her way. Emerging from the trees onto the sloping shore, Chris dropped her bike and kicked off her sandals. She sat on the hill leading down to the water and looked out at the ocean.

Home. That was how she felt at Castaway Cove. She was home in a way that was deeper than her feeling for her own house. The moonlight danced over the waves, seeming to welcome her.

Her mind whirled, trying to sort out the events of the last few days. *Why do I feel so bad?* she wondered. It was Bruce—but more than Bruce, too. It was the phoniness, the lies. It seemed to be everywhere. Miss Peabody appeared to be Miss Efficiency, but she was only pretending. In reality, the woman was so insecure that she panicked at the smallest thing. And though she was a bully, she was so terrified of getting into trouble that she was willing to lie about what she'd done.

It's not only Miss Peabody, though, thought Chris. She examined a strand of her hair in the moonlight. *This isn't me,* she admitted to herself. It would have been all right to bleach her hair if she'd done it to please herself. But she'd always liked her hair. She'd done it to look more like Jannette. Just like Miss Peabody, she was trying to be someone she wasn't.

That thought hit her hard. Could she be like Miss Peabody? No. She refused to believe that. But who was she? Really? It was so hard to know. How could she have been sure she wasn't the bleach-blond type unless she tried it?

"Aaaaahhhh!" Chris cried out. It was all too confusing!

Down at the water's edge, she stuck her feet in. It was warm and the swirling water felt good. Alone like this at the cove, she knew exactly who she was. She was Christine Amanda Brown, age fourteen. Like the crabs and the fish, she was a creature on earth. It didn't even seem so bad that she was a little overweight.

Why couldn't she feel that way back in the other world? *Because no one lets you, that's why*, she answered her own question. There were always TV commercials and magazine ads telling people they needed to look a certain way. And it seemed like everyone believed it. *Life is a great big costume party*, she thought dismally. *A party where everyone pretends to be someone they saw in an ad—an ideal person who probably doesn't exist at all.*

Chris turned to her left, in the opposite direction of the main beach. Almost no one ever went this way because the shoreline became rocky, and tangled bushes and vines spilled over onto the narrow beach. Chris wasn't sure why she headed this way. Maybe she wanted to walk as far away from people as she could get. She walked for almost fifteen minutes.

Suddenly, though, she heard a sound. Her heart leapt into her throat. Standing motionless, she listened. There it was again. It sounded as if someone or something was slapping the water.

Then, something caught her eye. Chris's hand flew to her mouth in fearful surprise. A large, dark mass was rolling in the surf.

The next sound she heard went right through her, sending a chill up her spine. It was a low, eerily familiar squeal. She'd heard it before—but where? Again she heard the slapping sound. This time it was followed by a sort of sputtering.

All at once, Chris realized what was in the water. Nervously she waded in, approaching the black form. "It *is* you," she whispered when she was close enough to see.

There before her, lying in less than three feet of water, was a bottle-nosed dolphin.

A series of low, pained squeaks greeted her. It was clear enough that the dolphin shouldn't have been in such shallow water, parted from the other dolphins. There was no doubt in her mind that this was Scamp, the dolphin who'd been hit by the boat.

He slapped the water once again with his broad, fluked tail. A small wave rolled in and washed over the exposed hump of his back. "Hi, Scamp," Chris said gently. "Don't worry, I'm here. You'll be okay." Cautiously she reached into the water and stroked the dolphin's nose.

Chris tried to recall what she knew of dolphins. She figured that for now, he was probably in a reasonably good spot. The water was deep enough to keep him wet, but shallow enough that he could breathe. But for how long? Glancing up at the shore, she guessed that the tide was out. When it came in, would it close over the dolphin and drown him?

She was torn. Obviously she had to go get help, but she hated to leave the dolphin. What if the tide began to go in while she was away? What if she couldn't find him again?

Scamp lifted his head weakly and gazed at her with listless eyes. *He looks scared*, thought Chris, patting him. "I hate to leave you," she told him. "But I have to go get help."

Wading out of the water, she noticed a point of light coming toward her down the shoreline. Too concerned about Scamp to be afraid, Chris ran toward the light and realized there were two figures outlined in the moonlight.

"I think I see her!" Liza's familiar voice called. Immediately, Liza and Sam ran toward Chris.

"Are you okay?" cried Sam, shining the flashlight on Chris.

"I'm okay," said Chris breathlessly, squinting. "But, listen. Remember that dolphin that was injured? I've found him."

"Found him?" gasped Liza. "Where?"

"Just down the beach," Chris told her. "He's swimming in shallow water. I think he's injured or sick. We have to help him. And fast, before the tide comes in."

Chapter Fourteen

Chris knelt in the water beside Scamp, tenderly stroking his side. Sam had left her with the flashlight while she and Liza went back to get help. *I hope they hurry,* she thought. The water was definitely rising. It was already to her waist.

"So the Professor told Gilligan that maybe he could make fuel by combining coconut milk with palm oil," she continued the story she'd begun telling Scamp. "If that worked, then they could put it in the boat and finally get off that dumb island." As an expert in TV trivia and a fan of *Gilligan's Island*, which she watched in reruns, she knew quite a few of these stories. Somehow, it seemed to her that it might comfort the dolphin if she kept talking. Or maybe it comforted her. She wasn't sure, and it didn't matter.

"So you see, Scamp," she concluded her story. "You're not the only one who's ever been stranded. All those people were stuck on the island and they didn't give up hope." A small wave washed over Scamp and Chris saw the blowhole on the top of his body close over. When the wave subsided, it opened again. The dolphin turned his head and looked at her sadly. "Help is coming," she told him hopefully. Scamp looked back at her and squealed as though he were trying to thank her. "Save your strength, pal," she said.

As she spoke, she noticed the black figure of someone coming toward her. "Chris," he called. "It's me, Bruce."

Bruce. When she'd dreamed of being alone with him, this was the last situation she could have ever imagined. She shined the flashlight on him and saw that he wore a white T-shirt and a pair of surfing jams she recognized as Lloyd's. "I figured you might need some help," he said as he waded into the water. "It's a little spooky out here in the middle of the night."

"It is. Thanks," she said. He was right. She suddenly felt less frightened and desperate now that he was there.

"Poor guy," he said, looking down at Scamp. "Sam said he got hit with a boat or something?"

"I don't see a cut, but it might be under him or something," said Chris. "Did Sam and Liza get help?"

"I think Sam's dad was trying to get a hold of some people he knows at the aquarium," Bruce told her. "Sam and Liza didn't tell everyone because they figured it wouldn't be good to have a whole swarm of people down here. Liza told Eddie, so he could keep an eye on the party. And I told Jannette where I was going. She's getting some food together and she'll join us."

"Okay," Chris said. Normally Bruce's last statement would have made her mad. But now it wasn't as important as saving Scamp.

"Is it my imagination, or is the tide coming in?" she asked.

"It's definitely coming in," Bruce said. "The water shouldn't cover him completely, right?"

"Right. He has to be able to get air through his blowhole," said Chris. "If he stays in this spot, and the water rises much more, he might drown. Do you think we could push him up into shallower water?"

"Maybe," said Bruce. "He's awfully heavy but we could try." When the next wave came in, Bruce tried to push Scamp up toward shore. The dolphin let out a low squeal. Bruce looked at Chris and shook his head. "Heavy isn't the word. This guy isn't budging."

"I'll help you next time," said Chris. As the next wave rolled over Scamp, Chris tucked the flashlight under her armpit and put all her weight into pushing the dolphin forward. Her feet slid in the sand, but she thought Scamp moved. She looked questioningly at Bruce.

"He moved," the boy answered her unspoken question. "We'll just push with all our strength on each wave and hope for the best."

"Looks like we could have used a whole swarm of people, after all," said Chris as the next wave rolled in. She pushed with all her might and Scamp inched forward. They kept this up for what seemed like a half-hour.

"Here comes a big one," Bruce warned, leaning into the dolphin, preparing to push. Chris helped but the wave was high and she fell into the water, bumping her nose on the dolphin's side.

When she got up she could see a speck of light underwater where she'd dropped her flashlight. It flickered and then went out. In the moonlight she could see Bruce, but Scamp was gone.

She stepped forward and stumbled into the dolphin. Groping in the dark water, she realized that Scamp was right at her feet. But he was underwater. "He's going to drown!" she cried.

"Stay calm," Bruce said in a shaky voice. "Dolphins can swim underwater for a long time. He's not going to drown that quickly." He kneeled down and threw his shoulder into the dolphin's side. "I think he's wedged against a sand bar," Bruce said in a low, grunting voice.

Chris pushed with him. Unexpectedly a large wave caught them from behind and sent Chris flying forward. The added water buoyed the dolphin. As she fell, she felt Scamp slide ahead of her.

Sputtering, she came up for air and saw the dolphin had been swept almost two yards closer to shore. "Good one," said Bruce, pushing his wet hair off his forehead. "That should hold us for a while." They walked closer to the dolphin, who lay there quietly. Suddenly he slapped the water with his back fluke as if to tell them he was still hanging in there.

"He's a fighter. I can tell," Chris said to Bruce.

"I hope so," Bruce replied. The sound of a boat's engine was getting increasingly louder and the water was suddenly illuminated. Chris and Bruce turned to see that a medium-sized cruiser had turned a corner and was coming at them from the left. From the direction of the cove, another smaller boat approached.

Immediately Chris and Bruce began calling to the boat. "We're here! Over here!"

The boat that had come in from the left shined another bright light onto Chris and Bruce. Blinded at first, Chris quickly saw that it was Mr. O'Neill's boat. She saw Liza and Sam standing on the deck, dressed in bathing suits. "How's he doing?" Sam called. Not waiting for an answer, she jumped off the boat. Liza followed her into the water and the two girls swam in to Chris and Bruce.

"Is Jannette with you?" Bruce asked Sam and Liza.

"No, she said she'd be down in a little while," Liza replied, bending to pet Scamp.

"Who's in the other boat?" Chris asked.

"A guy my father knows who's a vet and works in the aquarium up in Paradise Bay. His name is Tom Miles. He called the aquarium, and they'll send a boat down as soon as they can," Sam answered.

As they spoke the smaller boat moved closer and a short, muscular man appeared at the back of the boat. Chris saw him anchor and pull off his shirt before jumping from the side. He swam a short way to Mr. O'Neill's boat and spoke with Sam's father from the water. Mr. O'Neill threw what looked like a coil of rope into the water. Dr. Miles caught it and began swimming toward the shore.

"Where's the patient?" Dr. Miles asked when he was close enough. Chris immediately felt relieved by his calm voice.

"He's right here, but he's underwater," Bruce explained. Dr. Miles threw one end of his rope to Bruce. "Let's get this guy up so I can have a look at him," he said. He instructed Bruce and the girls on how to create a harness for the dolphin. Scamp resisted, slapping the water with his tail and twisting his body as they passed the rope back and forth. The hardest part was getting the rope under him, which they did by passing it under his tail and sliding it down. When it was done, Bruce swam the end of the rope out to Mr. O'Neill. Slowly, Bruce and Mr. O'Neill pulled the dolphin through the water, to the boat, with Dr. Miles swimming alongside.

Chris, Sam and Liza swam right behind Scamp and the vet. Treading water by the boat, they watched Bruce and Mr. O'Neill hoist the dolphin up along the boat, suspending him so that his blowhole was just out of the water.

"What happens now?" asked Chris.

"We met Dr. Miles on the dock," said Liza. "He said he has medicine, and splints and stuff in a waterproof bag. He even has a bucket of squid that are full of antibiotics. Dolphins love to eat squid, so if Scamp has an infection the antibiotics will cure it."

"So now everything will be fine?" asked Chris, suddenly feeling weary and chilled from being in the water.

"He said he wasn't sure," Sam answered. "He said they don't know much about why dolphins strand themselves. He said that lots of times they come ashore to die."

Chapter Fifteen

Once Scamp had been secured to the side of the boat, Dr. Miles put on snorkeling equipment and got into the water beside him. With the help of a bright underwater light, he examined the dolphin and discovered a wide gash just below his left flipper.

"He probably lost a fair amount of blood before this thing healed," the doctor surmised, climbing back aboard. "It looks infected to me. Maybe rust or something from the boat's blade got in there when he was hit. Sometimes an infection can interfere with their sonar. He may have become separated from the others that way." As he spoke, Dr. Miles took a bucket of squid from the corner of the boat. "Or he could have simply become too weak to find food, and swam ashore because he knew he couldn't go on."

He picked up one of the slippery creatures by its long, curving tentacle. "Those are full of antibiotics?" Chris asked.

Dr. Miles nodded. "I injected them before I came out." He repositioned his snorkeling mask over his eyes. "I hope the aquarium guys get out here soon, though. I'm just making do. They're more fully equipped." Once again the vet jumped into the water. Mr. O'Neill handed him the bucket of squid. Chris and the rest watched over the side as he fed them to Scamp.

A weak squeak came from Scamp for the first time in a while, and once again he slapped the water with his tail as he gulped down the squid. "I guess he was hungry," Liza noted.

"Look at that face," said Chris. "He looks so scared and lost."

"I know," Sam agreed. "Like a little kid who gets separated from his mother at a department store."

When the squid were gone, Dr. Miles climbed back on board. "Hopefully that will have some effect, but we need lots more. I hope those folks get here soon," he said.

For the rest of the night, Chris, Sam, Liza and Bruce sat aboard Mr. O'Neill's boat. They took turns sleeping on the hard, narrow cushions below deck—except for Chris. She didn't want to leave Scamp, so she sat by the side of the boat and spoke gently to him. "See? I told you help would arrive. You're going to be just fine. Would you like to hear the story of how Thurston Howell the Third and Gilligan rescued a chimp?"

At five-thirty, Sam and Liza were asleep. Dr. Miles had taken his boat back to shore to stock up on supplies, and Mr. O'Neill was talking over his radio to the Coast Guard.

Bruce was keeping watch with Chris. Their arms slung sleepily on the side of the boat, they gazed down at Scamp. "Too bad this had to happen to a nice dolphin and not Miss Peabody," he said.

"You know something, Bruce," Chris replied, not taking her eyes off Scamp. "Somehow Miss Peabody and the Palm Pavilion seem very unimportant right now. I mean, it's only a job, and Miss Peabody is just a silly woman who covers up her own unhappiness by making other people miserable."

"You're probably right," he agreed.

"Scamp is just the opposite," Chris continued. "He's so beautiful and sweet. I can't stand to see him lying there so weak. I bet he doesn't understand what's happening to him at all."

"You really feel close to him, don't you?" Bruce observed.

Chris nodded. "I don't know why. It's strange, isn't it?"

"Maybe it's because you're both kind of natural," said Bruce seriously.

"What do you mean?" asked Chris.

"Both of you are what you are. There's no phoniness about you." He chuckled. "I guess a dolphin wouldn't know how to be phony. Somehow I don't think that you would know, either."

Chris was moved by the gentle sincerity in his voice.

"That's a nice thing to say," Chris told him, looking up from the dolphin for the first time.

"It's what I think," he said. The sun was rising, streaking the sky with gold and pink. In the delicate light his face looked more handsome than she'd ever seen it. He smiled and for a moment she thought he was going to lean forward and kiss her.

The spell was broken by Mr. O'Neill. "The Coast Guard is escorting the aquarium folks out right now," he reported. "Dr. Miles is coming back with them."

Sam and Liza came onto the deck, looking dazed and half asleep. "Hey, I think I see Mom on the beach," Sam yawned.

Liza rubbed her eyes and looked. "Eddie's with her, and there's Lloyd and Greta."

Onshore, Mrs. O'Neill waved a red thermos at them. "Why don't you swim in and get some breakfast," Mr. O'Neill suggested to the kids. "I'll wait here with Scamp."

"I'd rather stay," said Chris.

"Come on," Sam urged her as she peeled off the sweat shirt she wore over her bathing suit. "You can come back later."

"You must be zonked," said Liza, swinging her long legs over the side of the boat.

"You're right," Chris agreed. She followed Sam, Liza and Bruce into the water. The four of them swam ashore, where Mrs. O'Neill greeted them with rolls, hot tea and juice. Chris was surprised at how hungry she was. Without a thought to her diet, she wolfed down a roll.

"How was our party?" Sam asked Greta as she sipped her tea.

"Those kids wouldn't go home," Greta complained. "I had to play Dad's tape of Irish sea tunes before they got the message."

"Jannette was supposed to come back with food," said Bruce. "I wonder what happened to her."

"She was at the party until the end," said Lloyd, munching on his second roll.

"Oh," said Bruce, sounding disappointed.

"You look beat," said Eddie, putting a towel over Liza's shoulders. "I have my brother's car. Why don't I drive you guys home?"

"That sounds good," yawned Liza. "I'm exhausted."

"Me, too," said Sam, getting to her feet. "Come on, Chris."

"You go, I want to stay," Chris insisted. "I'll be fine."

Bruce left with Eddie and the girls. Chris watched with Mrs. O'Neill, Lloyd and Greta as a large Coast Guard ship came into view, escorting a much smaller boat with the words "Paradise Bay Aquarium" written on the side.

She saw Dr. Miles jump into the water with two other people. This time, all three of them wore scuba gear. The people on the aquarium boat lowered a sturdy-looking platform into the water. The aquarium boat inched toward Mr. O'Neill's boat, where Scamp was still tied. In the water, the divers cut Scamp loose from his crude rope harness and moved him onto the platform. *That does look more comfortable*, thought Chris. Now

Scamp could rest and they'd be able to lower and raise him as the water level changed.

"Come on, Chris, sweetie," said Mrs. O'Neill. "Let's go home. They have this under control."

"Home!" cried Chris suddenly. "My mother is going to murder me. She must be worried sick."

"I called her. I called her," Mrs. O'Neill laughed. "I told her what happened and that you'd be with Mr. O'Neill and me."

"Thank you a million times." Chris breathed a sigh of relief.

"Thought you were going to be grounded until college, huh," laughed Lloyd.

"I would have been," Chris agreed, scrambling to her feet. She was reluctant to leave Scamp, but she knew he was getting the help he needed. She followed the others back to Mr. O'Neill's van. When they dropped her home she was so tired she could barely make it to the door.

"Christine, are you all right?" asked her mother, who was still in her robe having coffee. "Mrs. O'Neill told us—your hair! What have you done to it?"

"Could you punish me later, Mom?" Chris asked. "I'm so tired."

Her mother got up and put her arm around Chris. "All right. Sleep now. We'll talk later."

Chris went to her room, took off her rumpled clothes and flopped face down on her bed. She fell into a deep, dreamless sleep. When she woke up, every muscle in her body ached. At first, she wasn't sure why. Then she remembered pushing Scamp into shore with Bruce.

Although her head pounded, she had to find out what was happening with Scamp. A golden sunset streamed through her window. *I can't believe I slept all day*, she thought.

Quickly brushing her hair back, she pulled on a T-shirt and shorts. "Where are you going?" asked her mother when Chris emerged from her bedroom.

"I want to see what's happening with Scamp," Chris told her.

"Sam called," said her mother. "She said to tell you that there was nothing new. They were still giving him antibiotics and he was showing a few signs of improvement. But that's all."

"I have to go. Please, Mom," she begged. "I'll be home in an hour. Two hours tops."

"All right," her mother gave in. "But we still have to talk about that hair."

When Chris got to Castaway Cove it was getting dark. She made her way through the shadowy grove of palms and walked down the shore. A number of people were standing around. Apparently word had gotten out that there was a stranded dolphin in the area.

Heading toward her she saw Liza and Eddie, holding hands and walking in the water. They looked tired and sad. "How is he?" Chris asked them.

"Not too hot," said Eddie. "He's definitely more alert, but he's not swimming off that platform."

"The aquarium people are saying that if he doesn't swim free by tomorrow, they're going to take him to the Paradise Bay aquarium," Liza added sadly.

105

"Scamp can't be in an aquarium!" Chris cried. "Not Scamp. He needs the whole ocean to explore." Chris wasn't sure how she knew this, but she did. "I have to go see him."

"Forget it," Liza told her. "You can hardly see anything. They've moved him to the other side of the boat. We probably won't ever see him again—unless he ends up in the aquarium."

Chapter Sixteen

"I can't believe it's already September first," said Chris's father from behind his newspaper.

"Huh?" asked Chris, staring blankly into the refrigerator. "Oh, yeah, September."

"Got something on your mind?" Mr. Brown asked, putting down his paper.

"Scamp, that injured dolphin," she told him. "I want to know how he is. I can't stop worrying about him."

Sunday night she'd come home from the cove and told her parents everything that had happened. "And staying up all night with the dolphin turned your hair bleached blond?" her father had asked ironically. At that moment, Chris thought they were about to start dishing out punishments, but her parents simply told her that next time they assumed she would be more attentive to their rules.

After breakfast Chris immediately headed down to Castaway Cove. She had to try to see Scamp. That night, as she'd sat with him in the dark water, she felt as if they'd formed a bond. She'd been the one to assure him everything would be all right. And that was a kind of promise. Now she had to see it through.

When she got to the spot where she'd first found Scamp, the only boat out there was the aquarium boat. There was no one on the beach. *I guess most people went back to work today,* she figured.

Shielding her eyes against the sun, she looked out to the boat. Liza had been right. They'd turned so that Scamp was facing out to sea and she couldn't see if he was still on the platform.

Pulling off the shorts and T-shirt she wore over her bathing suit, she waded into the water. She had never been a strong swimmer, and the boat was about a quarter mile out, but she was determined to reach Scamp if he was there.

As she neared the boat, she became nervous that they might chase her if they spotted her. Chris rounded the front of the boat. The platform hung off the side—but it was empty.

Her heart pounded. Where was he? Had they taken him to the aquarium already? Had he died? Chris treaded water, not knowing what to do. She should never have left. She'd let him down.

Just then a man in scuba equipment popped up toward the back of the boat. "Get out of here, kid," he cried after removing the black plastic mouthpiece from his mouth.

"What happened to the dolphin?" Chris asked boldly.

"We're trying to help him and we don't need sight-seers," he answered brusquely.

"He's alive then!" Chris cried happily.

Another man appeared and pushed up his diving mask. It was Dr. Miles. "It's okay, Frank," he told his companion. "I know this young lady. She's the one who found the dolphin."

"Hi," said Chris, swimming toward him. "What's happening?"

Dr. Miles signaled her to look for herself. At the back of the boat, Scamp swam in a small pattern. He lifted his head and chattered a high squeaky greeting.

"He looks great!" Chris said, filled with relief.

"He's much better," Dr. Miles agreed. "He swam off the platform yesterday around five, but he won't leave the side of the boat. I don't know if it's because he's still too weak, or if his sense of direction is not what it was. For all our research, we know so little about what makes these guys tick."

"Maybe he's afraid," Chris suggested. "Dolphins don't usually travel by themselves, do they?"

"That could be, too," said Dr. Miles. "Though a dolphin's sonar is so acute that he'd probably locate another pod easily enough. The Coast Guard radioed us that they'd spotted a group about a hundred miles south of here. They may even be the same ones he was traveling with."

Frank pulled himself up the ladder on the back of the boat. Dr. Miles followed. "Come aboard," he invited Chris. "We're going to feed Scamp now."

As Dr. Miles tossed down antibiotic-filled fish, Chris realized that Scamp wasn't as exuberant as before. Still, he stuck his head up and squealed enthusiastically. He was able to catch the fish in his short, spiky teeth. "He'll be fine if he just gets up the nerve to leave," the doctor noted, throwing down another fish.

"What if he doesn't?" Chris asked as she threw a third fish down to the dolphin.

"Then he goes to the aquarium." Dr. Miles smiled kindly when he saw Chris's expression. "The aquarium isn't a prison. He'll be safe and well cared for. He may even star in a dolphin show."

"I know," Chris admitted glumly. "But it wouldn't be the same. A tank can never be the ocean."

Dr. Miles tossed down another fish and didn't speak for a moment. He seemed to study the dolphin. "You're right," he said finally. "It's not the same."

Chris spent the next two hours on the boat. The crew tried traveling out a half mile or so to see if Scamp would follow them into deeper water. But the animal stayed where he was, swimming within a small radius of the same spot.

"Why can't he just stay here?" Chris asked.

"For one thing, he'd starve," Dr. Miles said, rubbing his glasses on a towel. "We can't stay here and feed him forever, and this cove doesn't attract the kind or number of fish he needs."

At four o'clock, Scamp still hadn't moved from the tight pattern he was swimming. "I'm calling the aquarium," said Frank gruffly. "Maybe they'll want to airlift him."

Chris thought of Dolly Wanamaker, screaming and terrified as she was lifted into the helicopter. "Wait a while longer," she begged.

"I'm not sitting out here another day. The aquarium will be glad to get him," Frank said coldly.

Looking to Dr. Miles for help, she saw that he was not going to argue with Frank. Chis felt something inside of her sink like a lead weight. She'd never felt so beaten.

Then her eyes fell upon a cluster of cassette tapes lying on a narrow table. They were all classical, and she suddenly recalled a public television show she'd seen on whale strandings. Scientists didn't understand why it worked, but they'd brought an entire heard of beached whales back out to sea by playing the music of Brahms over a loudspeaker.

Quickly she began sorting through the tapes. "Those are my tapes, if you don't mind," said Frank.

"Have you got any Brahms?" she asked, still looking.

"I know what you're thinking, Christine," said Dr. Miles excitedly. He joined her in sorting through the tapes. "What's wrong with you, Frank? No Brahms?"

"Excuse me," quipped Frank, confused. "I didn't know we were having a music lovers' meeting."

"Let's try Vivaldi," said Dr. Miles to Chris. *The Four Seasons* has some pretty high-pitched notes." He turned to a large stereo box in the corner of the cabin. "You don't mind if we borrow this, do you?" he asked Frank.

"Knock yourself out," Frank replied.

Chris followed Dr. Miles out onto the deck. "I'll never make fun of Frank for being such a music maniac again," Dr. Miles said, turning the volume up to high.

A thin woman with sharp features and long brown hair walked out onto the deck. "This is Cynthia. She's the skipper of the boat," Dr. Miles introduced Chris to the woman.

Cynthia smiled at Chris. "What's up?" she asked Dr. Miles. "Frank told me you'd flipped out."

"No, no, we're experimenting," Dr. Miles explained. "Cynthia, when you hear the music go on, move out to sea as slowly as you possibly can. It's a long shot, but we have nothing to lose."

Chris cringed when the music came on, it was so loud. The boat sputtered to life and began moving at a crawl. Chris leaned over the side and saw Scamp pop his head out of the water and hold it there, obviously listening. "We've got his attention," she said hopefully. The music echoed through the air, the dramatic violins building to higher and higher levels of intensity.

But as the boat moved out, Scamp stayed where he was. One time he dove under and Chris prayed that he was following them. When he came up again, though, he wasn't far from the original spot. "It's not working, is it?" she said to Dr. Miles.

"It was worth a shot," he answered, disappointed. He bent to turn off the stereo, but Chris grabbed his arm.

"Keep it playing," she said urgently. Scamp had gone under a second time. She couldn't be sure, but she thought she could see his long gray body racing toward them under the water.

And then, as though shot from a cannon, Scamp breached high into the air. "Yes!" Chris cried out.

"All right!" shouted Dr. Miles. Frank and two other crew members who'd been watching from the cabin came running out, applauding wildly.

Chris didn't even know when she'd started crying, but her cheeks were soaked. Scamp breached another time as the music played around him. *He's dancing*, thought Chris. *He's dancing for joy. The joy of being alive.*

Chapter Seventeen

Chris came home that evening and immediately called
Sam and Liza. "You're a genius!" cried Liza when Chris
told her about the classical music.

When she called Sam, she already knew that Scamp
was okay from her father, who'd spoken to Dr. Miles.
"He told my father that you really took charge of the
situation. He was totally impressed," Sam told her. "I
wish you hadn't quit the Palm," she added sadly. "I
already miss seeing you there every day. Why don't you
just ask for your job back?"

Chris thought about it. "Miss Peabody probably
wouldn't even speak to me. It's no use."

That night Chris tossed in her bed. She dreamed she
was swimming through the ocean, underwater. It was a
wild, exhilarating feeling. In her dream she was swimming with dolphins. She saw Scamp, and she could
understand his squeals. He was singing, "This is life.
This is life," over and over in a joyful song.

In the morning, Chris awakened, almost surprised to be in her own bed. The dream of swimming with the dolphins had been so real—and so wonderful. Sitting forward, she thought about Scamp. It had taken courage for him to venture back out into the sea alone. Was he frightened of boats now? Would he ever come as close to one again, now that he'd had a bad experience?

She wondered why he hadn't wanted to go back at first, and what had changed his mind. Maybe the exciting music had reminded him of the pleasures of the open sea, despite the dangers. She'd probably never know. Dr. Miles had told her that even the scientists were still guessing.

Chris joined her parents in the kitchen. "What are you going to do today?" asked her mother.

"I'm not sure," Chris answered thoughtfully as she poured herself some orange juice.

"You sound as though you're toying with an idea, though,"her father observed, looking up from his paper.

"I am," she admitted. "I really want my job back. I was thinking of going over to the hotel and asking for it." She hadn't wanted to quit in the first place. She'd let Miss Peabody force her into that decision, and she'd felt powerless to correct her mistake. But yesterday had changed her mind. Scamp would be in an aquarium now if she hadn't taken action then. And she was going to take action now.

"Do you think they'll give it to you?" asked her father.

"If I don't try, I'll never know," she said. "I mean, yesterday I managed to help save a dolphin. I should be able to get a simple little job back, especially when I didn't do anything wrong in the first place."

"That's my girl," her mother said. "Give it your best shot."

Chris tried not to think too much as she rode toward the Palm Pavilion. If she did, she might lose her nerve. She parked her bike at the rack next to Sam's and Liza's, then walked in the front entrance of the hotel. She was immediately reassured to see Mrs. Chan back behind the front desk. But the next sight she saw made her hopes sink.

Miss Peabody stood in the middle of the lobby beside Mr. Parker. He looked the same, only tanner and less frazzled. Miss Peabody was talking to him excitedly, and Chris wondered if she was telling him about the episode with the Wanamaker twins.

Chris took a deep breath and approached the two of them. "Speak of the devil," said Miss Peabody when she saw Chris.

"Miss Brown," Mr. Parker greeted her. From his tone, she couldn't tell if he was glad to see her or not. "As I had anticipated, I left the tranquillity of my vacation only to return to a whirlwind of chaos. Furthermore, I am no less surprised to find you at the center of it."

"That's what I wanted to talk to you—" she began.

Mr. Parker held his hand up to silence her. "I don't care why you're here. I am simply glad that you are here."

"You are?" she questioned, confused.

"Yes. The Wanamakers decided to extend their stay,

and Mrs. Chan informs me that those two red-haired moppets have been whining for you to be their sitter."

"They have?" said Chris happily.

"Heaven knows why, after what you put them through," added Miss Peabody.

Uh-oh, thought Chris. *Now she's going to start telling all her lies. Mr. Parker is bound to believe her.*

To Chris's surprise, however, Mr. Parker turned his famous icy stare in Miss Peabody's direction. "My dear woman," he said sternly, "Mrs. Wanamaker has filled me in on the details of that sordid display of hysteria. I must tell you that while anyone might panic in a crisis, I find it reprehensible that you would try to pass off the culpability for your actions on this young girl."

Huh? thought Chris. *I wish he would speak plain English.*

"Speaking more plainly," Mr. Parker continued, as if reading Chris's thoughts, "I want you out of my hotel today, Miss Peabody. Since I walked in this morning, I have heard nothing but complaints about how you've terrorized my staff. And another thing . . ." As Mr. Parker continued to speak his mind, Chris caught sight of Sam and Liza coming in the back door of the lobby with two toddlers. They spotted Chris right away and headed toward her.

"The Highcourt Group will not be pleased with your attitude," Miss Peabody said in a high, shrill voice.

"The Highcourt Group will be hearing from me personally today," Mr. Parker countered. "I will not have

117

my hotel staff demoralized simply to satisfy your corporate ambitions."

"You can't speak to me like this!" Miss Peabody shrieked.

"Madam, I do not normally resort to name-calling," said Mr. Parker. "But let me leave you with this thought. If we were in India, you would be sacred."

It took Chris a moment, then she got it. Cows were sacred in India. He was calling Miss Peabody an old cow. Apparently Miss Peabody made the connection immediately. Turning crimson with fury, she turned and stormed away.

"Yeaahhhh!" Liza and Sam burst into applause, standing behind Mr. Parker.

Mr. Parker turned on them sharply. A quick grin brightened his sharp face, and then he resumed a serious expression. "Are you without something to do, Miss Velez? Miss O'Neill?"

"No, sir," said Liza, still smiling. "We just brought the kids in to use the bathroom."

"Does this mean I can come back to work?" asked Chris.

"Apparently so. The Wanamakers requested you this morning. Go ask Mrs. Chan if they are still in their rooms."

"Thank you, Mr. Parker. And welcome back," she said. "It's great to see you again."

Mr. Parker's brows furrowed. "Yes, well, thank you, Miss Brown. It is not altogether unpleasant to be back. Now, if you'll excuse me, I had better call the Highcourt

Group and cover my posterior as best I can." With a quick nod, he left.

"You're back!" cried Liza, jumping up and down ecstatically.

"Wow! Parker really came through," said Sam. "No more Miss Peabody! What a relief!"

"Yeah," agreed Chris. "Everything's the way it was. Mr. Parker is back and so is Mrs. Chan. Scamp is okay. And I'm a Palm Pavilion employee again. It's as if last week never happened."

"Not exactly," said Liza, her eyes twinkling merrily. "We heard Bruce and Jannette having an argument this morning. He was ticked off that she never came with the food the way she promised."

"I heard him tell her that you were out there being so brave, and the least she could have done was show up," added Sam.

"He said that? He thought I was brave?" Chris said, thrilled by Sam's words.

"Ask him yourself," said Liza with a nod of her head. Chris followed Liza's gaze and saw Bruce standing off by one of the mahogany pillars, as if waiting to speak with her. "Go talk to him," Liza urged. "We have to get these kids to the john before they burst. We'll meet you back here."

She walked toward Bruce. "Hi," she said. "I got my job back."

"That's terrific," he said. "I missed seeing you every day."

"Thanks," Chris replied, suddenly shy.

"I'm not just saying it," he told her. "I didn't realize until you quit that I sort of took talking with you for granted."

Chris loved the way this conversation was going. Was he trying to say that he liked her? Liked her . . . as in romance?

"I feel like I really got to know you that night with Scamp," he continued. "It's weird how things change. I always thought Jannette was so nice, but I saw a different side of her that night. And I saw a different side of you, too."

"What did you see in me?" Chris dared to ask.

"I saw someone who can care about more than just herself," he answered. "Would you mind if I called you later? Tonight maybe?"

"I would love that," she replied.

"Good. We'll figure out what we want to do then, okay?"

"Okay," she replied.

He smiled at her. "Well, I'd better get back out to the pool. Talk to you later."

As she watched him walk away, Chris just grinned. He did like her! There was no doubt about it.

"Tell! Tell!" said Liza, running up to Chris, a toddler in her arms.

"Did he ask you out?" Sam wanted to know, holding the hand of her toddler.

"I think he's going to," Chris said excitedly.

Liza put the little girl down and pounded Chris's arm happily. "Do you think it's your new blond hair?"

"It isn't that at all. He said he likes *me*," Chris answered, bursting with happiness. "Me myself."

"Why shouldn't he?" said Sam. "We like you."

"Thanks," said Chris. "I like you guys, too." As they spoke, she noticed the Wanamaker twins coming into the lobby in identical red bathing suits. "I'd better go get those two. Meet you by the pool."

"Okay," said Sam.

"Welcome back," said Liza.

Crossing the lobby, Chris approached the twins and Mrs. Wanamaker. Yes, everything was pretty much the same as it had been before she quit. Then she thought of Scamp, and she knew she'd never be exactly the same again.

* * *

Sam is feeling a bit down—not to mention jealous of Chris and Liza—because she doesn't have a boyfriend. Then she meets the newest Palm Pavilion employee. He's a little old for her, but he'll do . . . won't he?

Watch for SITTING PRETTY #5: *Boy Trouble*

SUZANNE WEYN

Suzanne Weyn is the author of many books for children and young adults. Among them are: *The Makeover Club*, *Makeover Summer*, and the series NO WAY BALLET. Suzanne began baby-sitting at the age of thirteen. Later, while attending Harpur College, she worked as a waitress in a hotel restaurant. Suzanne grew up on Long Island, N.Y., and loves the beach. Sailing, snorkeling, water-skiing and swimming are some of her favorite activities. In SITTING PRETTY she is able to draw on these experiences.

Suzanne now has a baby of her own named Diana, who has two terrific baby sitters—Chris and Joy-Ann.